Rock-A-Bye Baby

The Sand Maiden
Book Two

L. R. W. LEE

eBook ISBN: 978-1370271443
Paperback ISBN: 978-1099000522
Woodgate Publishing

Table of Contents

Part I: Wake 6

Part II: REM 115

Part III: Nightmare 189

Appendix...224

DREAM REALM
NAVEREY
ANARIT
ECI
ELCICI
NEZORF
LEMNOS
SEA OF DREAMS
BERGAZ
AIARP
RIA
RETAW
ROLSE
ARRET
DOOW
ANATSA
ZUDAV
LETAM
ABUJ
ERABAB
ARCCA
ERIF
ERARAH
LUJNAB
LAPMUK

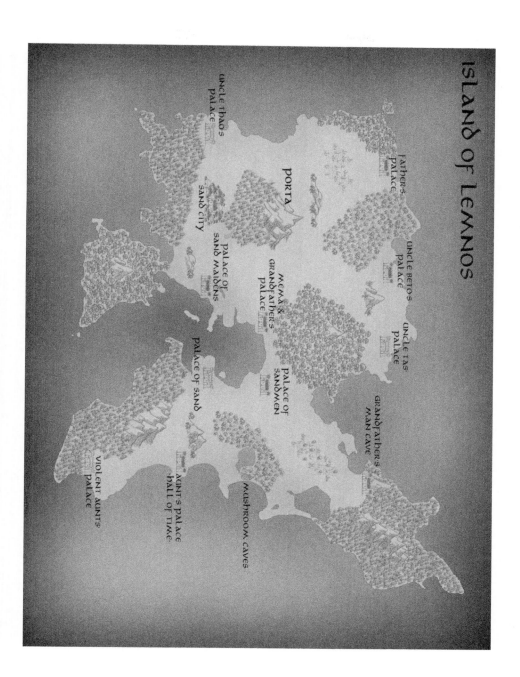

ISLAND OF LEMNOS

FATHER'S PALACE

UNCLE THAOS PALACE

UNCLE BETO'S PALACE

UNCLE TAS PALACE

PORTA

SAND CITY

MEMA & GRANDFATHER'S PALACE

PALACE OF SAND MAIDENS

PALACE OF SANDMEN

GRANDFATHER'S MAN CAVE

PALACE OF SAND

VIOLENT AUNTS PALACE

AUNT'S PALACE HALL OF TIME

MUSHROOM CAVES

Part I: Wake

Rock-A-Bye Baby

By Mother Goose
London Wake Realm

Rock-a-bye, baby, in the treetop,
When the wind blows the cradle will rock,
When the bough breaks the cradle will fall,
Down will come baby, cradle and all.

Baby is drowsing, cosy and fair,
Mother sits near in her rocking chair,
Forward and back, the cradle she swings,
Though baby sleeps, he hears what she sings.

Rock-a-bye baby, do not you fear,
Never mind, baby, mother is near,
Wee little fingers, eyes are shut tight,
Now sound asleep - until morning light.

Prologue

Long ago...

I'd never dreamed. None of us had.

But it didn't mean humans didn't need Father, the god of dreams, and Grandfather's, the god of sleep, help accomplishing the feat. My elders bore the marks—dark circles that marred the flesh beneath their eyes and frequent yawns—all because humans would quickly turn on each other, destroying the entire race, if they failed in their duties. No pressure.

Father had told tales of humans striking one another down with blades they'd conjured from thin air, vanishing ground from beneath other's feet, shredding obstacles with fierce winds, and more. Yes, humans certainly had the ability to kill and they'd no doubt do it if they didn't sleep and dream.

We'd no idea how Father and Grandfather accomplished it, but we revered their skill nonetheless. It's why I'd become particularly worried about both of them of late. They walked around as if in dazes. Gone were Grandfather's once beaming eyes and Father's booming laughter. How much longer could they last? They were running themselves ragged.

So, as we shared fortnight family dinner this morning—a tradition begun, and insisted upon, by Mema, the name we affectionately referred to Grandmother by, to keep our large family close—my stomach tightened when Grandfather forced a smile at his bride then patted Father's arm and rose from the head table that stood perpendicular to the two at which my siblings and I dined. Something was up.

The sun sent soft light through the floor-to-ceiling windows that lined one wall of the dining room, painting the otherwise stark white with a warm, pinkish hue. Our easy chatter quieted and I ricocheted looks between my siblings who wore furrowed brows. Several bit a lip. Mema schooled her expression and gave nothing away. Whatever it was, it couldn't be good.

Grandfather, the god of sleep, covered a yawn, paradoxical to be sure, then cleared his throat. "Over time, the number of humans in Wake has grown to the point that your father and I are wearing ourselves ragged trying to care for them. And their numbers just keep increasing. With such short lives, they multiply much more rapidly than we do, so their numbers will only continue to grow, exponentially even... and we can't keep up."

Such a dire prediction. My stomach twisted. So what were they going to do?

Grandfather continued, "We can see only one way to prevent calamity. We are offering to train any of you who want to learn our craft. We will transition what we do to those we train." His gaze traveled across us, no doubt checking our reactions.

That was their plan?

As the ninth daughter, the thirteenth child, of the god of dreams, I was accustomed to life as a royal princess. Mema had taught me and my twenty-one siblings the proper etiquette of our positions, and the most interesting goings on in my life to this point had been her requirement that we maidens do needlepoint, something I barely tolerated, and an occasional trip to the mushroom caves, something I loved. Never had Father or Grandfather asked for our involvement, but if I was understanding, life might get considerably more interesting.

No one said a word. My mind whirred.

"We are not requiring this, only offering this opportunity to those who want it. We will also make this offer to our subjects."

Father joined Grandfather, standing, and continued, "Because of the complex nature of our craft, anyone who wishes to pursue this will need to apprentice. We've also decided to appoint regents, one per province, to supervise and ensure humans continue to receive quality sleep and dreaming. They'll govern and ensure the needs of the various Dream regions are cared for. They will be selected from among the best apprentices. For those of you who volunteer, you will be assigned a human charge for his or her lifetime. Your training will focus on putting them to sleep as well as reviewing their thoughts and memories from a sun and weaving them into dreams."

I bit my lip, debating their offer. Could I learn everything they did to make humans sleep and dream? What if I screwed up? What if a human died because of me? I couldn't live with myself. My knee started bouncing under the table.

Another thought careened to the forefront of my mind. If enough of us helped, would Father and Grandfather be able to spend more time with us? I'd hardly seen anything of them of late.

I drew a hand to my mouth. Father. How I longed to see him more often. And if he was around more, might Mother come, too? She claimed her work in message delivery prevented her coming, but I questioned.

I glanced across my siblings. They'd say I was being sunshine and rainbows again if I voiced my hopes. Maybe I was naïve, but if we could have our family together... I drew in a deep breath and let it out slowly, ignoring the chill that ran down my back as I raised my hand. "I'll do it."

Everyone gave me long looks. I didn't care. I'd no idea what I was signing up for, but if it meant more time with Father and Grandfather, and possibly Mother, I'd do it.

I'd learn what they did and no human would come to harm.
How I prayed that was true.

Chapter One

The stars danced in the sky and I reached out to the dream canopy, to Drake, my current dream charge, to weave his dreams. He'd taken a fancy to a maiden of late. Ah, youth. I smiled wondering what thoughts I would discover and shepherd this night.

I furrowed my brow, wait, where was he?

I tried again to find him, to the same result. My heart climbed into my throat. I tried again. He'd always opened his mind to me right away, but I couldn't find him.

Panic bit into me. He'd been my charge for fourteen annums, I knew how to find him. I rechecked myself anyway, reaching my mind out to and through the dream canopy, picturing it: Water province. Voda City. Hexham Canal. Left at the second fountain. Third house on the right.

Only silence greeted me. Where was he? The last time this had happened... I couldn't think it. Wouldn't.

I flew out my door and down the hallway, clipping my wing on a corner. I spotted six of my sisters in the sitting room ahead, all occupied with their own charges. But I needed help.

"Velma, Eolande," I shouted.

Alfreda, an amicable older sister, must have heard the fear in my voice because she swooped to a stop in front of me. Her dream charge had reached eighty annums and 'gone on' a fortnight before. She was in the midst of her mourning moon. She grabbed my forearms and locked eyes. "Calm down. What's wrong?"

"I can't find Drake." The story spilled from my lips.

My sisters had done their best to console me, but just past sunrise, when a steward showed a uniformed officer into the sitting room, my stomach went hard. An inquisitor. They looked into unusual or suspicious goings on. I'd only ever seen them when something bad had happened.

Word had spread and all nine of my brothers and twelve of my sisters, as well as Mema, had assembled. The room was crowded with so many of us. Most stood silently, holding themselves, wings tucked tight. A few sat. All of us braced for the news.

The man drew his black wings in closer as he stopped. It was never a good sign. "Allow me to introduce myself. I'm Master Inquisitor Ulster. Which of you is Alissandra?"

I raised a hand where I sat on one of several divans, Velma, my eldest sister, to my left, Wynnfrith, my roommate, to my right.

Addressing me directly, the inquisitor said, "You were right to alert us when you couldn't connect with your dream charge. I regret to inform you that he met an untimely demise at the hands of fate. Collectors escorted him through the gates of Light realm not long ago. I'm truly sorry."

The words clanged in my head like a discordant bell tolling.

My stomach threatened to revolt. My worst fears had been confirmed. Tears overwhelmed the dam I'd struggled to hold them behind and Velma and Wynnfrith enveloped me in a hug.

What could possibly have happened? They never told us. Perhaps they never learned themselves. I doubted knowing would have eased my pain, but not knowing always made it feel that much more meaningless, especially when my charge had been so young.

Small consolation, Drake had gone to Light realm, a place of eternal peace and comfort for humans. I'd have been surprised if Shadow realm had won him, but you never knew until accounts were settled.

I took a deep breath trying to stop crying, then swiped a sleeve across my cheeks. Velma and Wynnfrith sat back but both kept a comforting hand on me.

I appreciated that my family didn't coddle and utter meaningless platitudes. We'd each been through this before with one dream charge or another and would continue to, on into eternity. I guess you could say it was a hazard of the trade. Some sandmaidens and sandmen, a few of my siblings included, kept their charges at a safe distance. Others put in their time like it was any other task, no different than sewing or studying. But it wasn't, not to me. I think they just tried to avoid feeling like this.

Those who tried to protect their hearts failed to understand that we got to make a profound difference in each of our charge's lives, especially when we stopped trying to protect ourselves and gave everything we had to shepherd and mould our charges as we wove their dreams. I always drew on personal experiences, the hard as well as the easy, when helping my charges work through their problems. The challenge to be authentic was what fueled my passion to do my very best. I only prayed I was worthy of the honor.

But as a result, I couldn't help growing attached to each human entrusted to me, damn the consequences. If it meant I felt this way every now and again, it was a small price to pay for the meaning and sense of fulfillment I gained.

Velma continued stroking my shoulder and I glanced over to Alfreda. As if understanding my unspoken question, a small smile escaped her. She seemed to be doing okay adjusting to the loss of her charge. But then, in my experience, closure usually came easier with the aged.

I poked at my breakfast as the sun set. Alfreda wrinkled her brow, watching me from down the table. Wynnfrith and Velma mimicked.

A fortnight had passed. I should have made progress mourning Drake's passing. I should have. But I hadn't.

It's not like I'd never lost a young dream charge. I had. But I'd been younger myself and questions of meaning hadn't plagued me. Not like this: What might Drake have become one day? What had the Ancient One's purposes for him been? How could it have been fulfilled so soon? Had it been? Or had something interfered? Was that even possible? These and other questions wouldn't allow me to settle, much less gain closure. Drake had changed me, no different than each of my past charges. And because of it, a part of him, like them, would live on eternally in me.

Across from me, Mema gave me a long look. "There's a set of twins, boys, soon to be born to Emperor Altairn and his wife. I planned to recommend Alfreda for one but hadn't yet decided on a sand being for the other."

I met her gaze.

"You still have a fortnight in your mourning moon. But—"

"Yes, please, yes, I'm ready." I'd never had a twin before. I pushed back my despair as the novelty reawakened me.

Mema lifted a brow, then took a bite of bubblefruit. She chewed slowly, watching me.

I drew my wings closer as I bit into a dreamberry muffin fresh from the oven, trying to prove how 'ready' I was. My sisters, seated around the table, continued their conversations, but their sparkling eyes directed at me, grins, and giggles behind drawn hands told me they not only heard but were excited for me.

"Very well, when I speak to your father later, I'll suggest you for the other."

"Thank you, Mema." I ate another muffin and a bubblefruit to underscore my claim.

A sense of meaning obliterated my despair and enthusiasm filled me once more. I'd have a twin as my next charge.

Mema rose and strode for the door. As soon as it snit shut, I wiped my mouth with my napkin. Just as I set it on my empty plate, Alfreda squealed and practically leapt from her chair.

She enveloped me in a hug. "I'm so excited. Twins, Ali. We'll share twins." She practically bounced.

My smile grew bigger still. "I know. We've never shepherded twins. I'm so happy. We'll get to do it together." I squeezed her hand.

"And princes," Wynnfrith said. "No doubt they'll be heartthrobs." A dreamy look crossed her eyes. "You'll have so much fun directing their love lives."

Alfreda and I snorted, then covered our mouths.

"Mema still has to ask Father," Velma said.

"Have you ever known him to deny anything Mema asks for?" Wynnfrith asked, raising a brow.

"I just don't want you to have your hopes dashed, Ali."

Sunshine and rainbows. I knew what she was thinking and I rolled my eyes. "Thank you for looking out for me, big sis, I love you for it, but I agree with Wynnfrith."

Velma smiled then stepped close and hugged me. "Then assuming Father approves, congratulations. I'm very happy for you, little sis."

Alfreda squeezed my hand harder.

A prince. What would he face in his lifetime? What would I help him work through? But first things first, he had to make it into the world and that in itself could be wrought with the worst dangers.

Chapter Two

Why, oh why, had I wanted another charge?

I'd been up all sun and felt like I walked in my sleep. I fanned away a yawn as I looked out the floor-to-ceiling window between my sister's and my bed. The sun was a glowing orange ball sinking down behind the horizon.

My downy soft covers called to me. I felt like lying down, but I couldn't. My new charge needed to sleep, some more. Coming into the world was fraught with peril and he needed to be a healthy size before his mother bore him. And the best way to accomplish that was to have him sleep—it's when he grew fastest.

I had work to do.

I reached my mind out to and through the dream canopy, and found him, and then his thought thread, that invisible connection every sand being shared with their charge that allowed us to see their thoughts. It waved erratically as it usually did, as if trying to attract my attention, making sure I couldn't miss it.

I envisioned taking step after careful step, making my way down the dark thread. When I reached the end, I found the strands where his thoughts flowed and sprinkled sand on them. Not too much. He was little.

Once he settled into sleep, I latched onto the strands. His thoughts started flowing in murky gray images: Something stroked his side—a pleasurable sensation—probably his mother's hand. I grabbed the thought and wove it into a dream. Sounds. Agreeable. Soothing. I threaded these together, too, and added them to the others. I continued capturing the sensations as he slept, until something jabbed his side, his brother's foot no doubt, and he woke.

I didn't blame him. It had gotten cramped with two of them occupying the space of one babe.

Grandfather was a twin. I couldn't picture him and crazy, morbid Uncle Thao sharing the same squished space.

How could twins exist like this? It seemed inhumane.

I bit my lip. Single babes had enough trouble entering the world. Would having two of them in the same cramped space, cause more? My stomach clenched.

To calm myself, I sang my charge his first lullaby.

Lullaby, and good night, in the skies stars are bright.
May the moon's silvery beams bring you sweet dreams.
Close your eyes now and rest, may these hours be blessed.
'Til the sky's bright with dawn, when you wake with a yawn.

Lullaby, and good night, you are mother's delight.
I'll protect you from harm, and you'll wake in my arms.
Sleepyhead, close your eyes, for I'm right beside you.
Guardian angels are near, so sleep without fear.

Lullaby, and good night, with roses bedight.
Lilies o'er head, lay thee down in thy bed.
Lullaby, and good night, you are mother's delight.
I'll protect you from harm, and you'll wake in my arms.

Lullaby, and sleep tight, my darling sleeping.

On sheets white as cream, with a head full of dreams.
Sleepyhead, close your eyes, I'm right beside you.
Lay thee down now and rest, may your slumber be blessed.

I fanned away another yawn and glanced over at Alfreda who sat half-awake on Wynnfrith's bed, across from me. Wynnfrith had surrendered to the chaos that new charges were, and had taken to sleeping in Deor's—Alfreda's roommate—room until our new charges had an established sleep schedule. Dark circles marred the area below her eyes and her raven hair was disheveled. She gave me a weary look. "I'm so glad we have each other this time. This stage is always a killer."

I nodded. "Couldn't agree more. Call me crazy, but I still love it. We get to be there from the very beginning, to connect with him or her. I feel like I get to know the very special human my charge will become."

Alfreda laughed. "Every one of your charges has been a special human?"

I furrowed my brow. "Of course, aren't yours?"

A smile mounted her lips. "In a way, I suppose."

"Do you think Mother felt this way about us when we were inside her?"

Alfreda gave me a long look. The question had always bothered me but I had never dared ask, any of my siblings. "If you mean do I think she sees each of us as someone special, I think her absence speaks volumes. You're not going to like me saying this, but I think we are the consequences of her and Father's... passion. Nothing more."

I frowned. "That's awfully harsh."

"Work is more important to Mother than us. And even though Father's retired, he still doesn't spend any more time with us."

I opened my mouth to object, but Alfreda raised a hand. "Mema's got lots going on working for Aunt Dite, yet she's always here for us."

I wanted to, but I couldn't argue.

"Ali, I used to let it get to me. It still makes me steam when I think about it, but there's nothing we can do to change it."

I sighed.

"We have each other." She smiled. "I'm a bit biased, but I think all my siblings are pretty special."

I squeezed her hand.

I still mulled over what Alfreda had said, moons later, but joy obliterated my melancholy after putting my charge to sleep and starting to monitor his thoughts.

"They've been born! He's waving his arms freely," I told my sister as she entered the sitting room.

She squealed, then bounced down on the sofa beside me and closed her eyes. I closed mine, too, and got to work.

Voices, people speaking to and about my charge, populated his thoughts. I marveled at the litany of names used to address him: Prince Kovis Rhys Aldrick Desmond Altairn. Good grief. Could they add any more? Longer than any of my charges before. But they'd named him Kovis. It was a good name.

"Oh, Ali!" Alfreda reached out and grabbed my arm. I met her eyes. "They named my charge Prince Kennan Griffin Darren Alden Altairn. Boy, so many hopes pinned to him." She shook her head, then went back to weaving.

So Kovis and Kennan, twins and all ours to shepherd.

"Aw…" I couldn't help myself. My charge was so sweet. Kovis sucked on Kennan's extended fist as his brother thrust it within reach of his mouth, or so his thoughts, this one a memory, revealed as he slept.

I often wished we had access to the whole of a charge's mind, but these snippets—memories he nursed, things he feared, desires he longed for and more, that occupied his thoughts as he slept—had to suffice. How much easier my task to weave dreams would have been if we could only look back at everything that had happened during the course of a sun, or all his memories for that matter. If only…

I pushed the foolish wish away and refocused on Kovis sucking his brother's fist. Speaking of which... I laughed.

Alfreda opened her eyes. "What is it?"

"Kovis figured out how exciting the sight of an abundant mound of flesh with a pink nipple is. He's fixated on them." I grinned, as I had with all of my previous charges. It meant Kovis would be a healthy boy. That fact always filled me with joy. He had a good shot at leading a long life. "I'll have fun weaving these dreams."

Alfreda chuckled. "That 'attraction' will no doubt last his lifetime if my past male charges are any indication."

I snorted in recognition and set about weaving that into Kovis's dreams.

When I had captured luscious pink mounds to my satisfaction, I watched the next bit of Kovis's thoughts play.

A sweet voice said, "We've brought your sons, Emperor. If I may, they are quite the little charmers."

A low voice boomed in reply, "I did my duty naming them, keep those murderers out of my sight."

"Yes... Yes, majesty."

I sucked in a breath. Murderers?

Chapter Three

Would Mother come? Would Father? I pinched the skin at my throat.

It was the Festival of Sandlings we would celebrate this sun, the celebration of new life. Yet my chest ached. I couldn't accept Alfreda's view that my siblings and I were nothing more than the consequence of Mother's and Father's passion. Factually, we were, but we had to *mean* something to them despite their regular absence from our lives. We had to. *I* had to.

New life was a promise for the future. And Mother and Father had created twenty-two of us promises.

"Why the long face?" Harding, a laid-back brother, asked, leaning over, beside me.

I shook my head. "Who are we missing?" I asked, trying to cover my melancholy.

A corner of my brother's mouth hitched upward. "All nine of us males are present and accounted for, little sister, but hum... I count only seven, eight, nine of my beautiful sisters. Why is it females always take longer to ready themselves?"

I swatted his arm. "Because we have to live up to ridiculous standards *set by you males*: curling our hair, painting our nails, prettying our faces, the list is endless. And that's on top of procuring couture dresses"—I held up my pointer finger—"with coordinating shoes…" I exaggerated looking his formal tunic and dress slacks up and down. "… that are different each and every time as well as the envy of our citizens."

He drew a hand to his chest and twitched his wings. "You exhaust me just listening to you."

"Mema and Grandfather haven't yet arrived, and it's their palace, so lighten up on we fair maidens." I brought my head down sharply.

Harding chuckled. "Mema and Grandfather are waving to the crowds from the balcony."

I opened my mouth and closed it quickly. Harding chuckled and gave me a one-arm hug.

Father's booming voice carrying down the hall outside the sitting room drew my attention and a smile to my face. I pulled my hands to my chest. He'd come.

Judging by his volume, he was at least in a mood befitting this occasion—an improvement over the last time I'd seen him. But when he stepped through the door with Mother on his arm, I understood why.

Mother had come. She'd come, too. My heart rose with happiness. I'd ask her to come back to our palace and chat afterward, just for a bit.

And Father was actually smiling. I never understood what he saw in Mother, beyond her beautiful looks—she was beautiful with her slim frame, long neck, and dimpled chin. As usual, she looked lovely in her elegant fuchsia gown that accented her curves in all the right places. I envied her. Her work in message delivery among the gods didn't require her to remain invisible like us and she took advantage of it, expressing herself in bold colors.

But Father was still interested in her. She'd had all twenty-two of us, yet he'd never married her, so what was it that kept them together? It had to be more than beauty, right?

Velma pecked Mother on the cheek, as did Wasila and Wynnfrith.

I stepped forward and drew my arms around her slight waist, breathing in her floral perfume. "It's good to see you again, Mother."

She patted my back and leaned back, then pushed a stray lock behind my ear. "You look lovely, dear."

Father gave me a wink. I hadn't realized how much I'd missed that until this heartbeat.

"Are we ready?" Father boomed, over the noise of our chatter. "Iris." He extended his elbow for Mother.

We headed out the door and turned left, walking toward the front of the palace. My grandparents loved sculptures and several pieces resided in wall niches of varying sizes down the length of the hall. My two favorites were a life-size female smiling down at the sandling she held, the other, only a few handbreadths tall, was of the Ancient One creating sand people and the other creatures that filled Dream—the sculpture captured the heartbeat when a sandstorm erupted in the cauldron of the skies and the Ancient One shaped the sand into humans, animals, sea creatures, every living thing, then tipped it over, and poured them all out.

The sun had dropped halfway to the horizon as we emerged onto the balcony that wrapped around most of the front of their palace. Grandfather and Mema were waving to the crowds, three floors below, who were clearly taking it all in with enthusiasm. The heartbeat Father's subjects saw us their cheering and celebrations grew even louder.

I beamed and waved between Challis and Harding from the far-left end of the line we'd formed, which traced the balcony's curve. My brothers kept a more dignified demeanor. Yes, I was always the excitable one, but so what; we were celebrating sandlings. They were our future, but I'd expanded this celebration to include Kovis. He wasn't immortal life, but he was new life, and deserved to be recognized.

Father took Mother's hand and they stepped to the marble railing, then waved.

She... they, looked good. Happy. Together.

Father raised his arms and called for silence. Once the crowd settled, he began. "Welcome to this joyous occasion, the Festival of Sandlings. We are glad you could join us here. We welcome those of you especially who have traveled far. You could have joined in festivities in your local areas but you made the extra effort to come here and celebrate with us."

Applause and hoots rose.

"This sun we celebrate our offspring, our future. As you may recall, Hypnos and I instituted these festivities after transitioning our duties to many of you. With ever-increasing numbers of humans, sandlings became the hope of our future."

Whistles pierced the silence.

"We appointed the vernal equinox—one of two suns per annum where light and dark are equal—for our celebration because sandlings brought Dream from the darkness we faced, to light, or a bright future reliably shepherding human sleep and dreams."

I scanned the crowds as he spoke. Sand people stretched nearly as far as I could see. Families were spending the sun here as evidenced by the myriad of blankets littering the ground with sandlings moving about or playing.

I watched one family, closer to the front. The woman held a babe in her arms. I couldn't make out her expression, but the image captivated me. She held new immortal life. Whether the couple had conceived the babe or Selova, our territory's dream stitcher, had crafted it, it didn't matter. This babe would live forever and make a life for him or herself. He or she might weave dreams, be a tradesperson, or pursue some other craft, but he was promise and possibility embodied, and the hope for Dream's future. As was Kovis for Wake's.

Yes, Kovis. I sighed. 'Murderers.' It's what his father had called him and his twin nearly a moon before. It had set me on edge and left me feeling uneasy since. I kneaded my hands. Why would the emperor say such a thing? How could a father say that about his own children? More importantly, where had Kovis's mother been? Why had she not intervened? These babes needed her love. I'd resisted the notion but had begun to wonder if she'd... abandoned them. I hated to admit I understood, but... My heart hurt. For them. Yes, for them. Mother had come.

Cheering interrupted my musings and I wiped a finger beneath my eyes. Stewards filed behind my siblings and me bearing cloth sacks brimming with small, wrapped packages.

"And now, allow us to show you a token of our joy," Father said.

I swallowed and took a deep breath. This was my favorite part of the sun, distributing gifts to sandlings so when they grew old enough to understand, their elders could show each one tangible proof of how much they were valued, by their sovereign, himself. So I, along with my sisters, bent over and cinched the string in the hem of our gowns.

Mother did the same. I covered my mouth with a hand. She planned to participate. She would *celebrate* sandlings, too.

"Go," Father called.

We all launched, servants trailing closely. I glanced over my shoulder. Mother flew, hand in hand with Father. He gave her a wink and she beamed. And my heart soared. I couldn't wait to have a good chat with her later.

I returned my attention to the families spread before me. Our guards formed a protective perimeter about us, but I never paid attention to them. I touched down beside the couple I'd spotted, and the servant handed me a gold-wrapped box. "May your babe grow strong and bless you."

The father bobbed his head. "May our kingdom prosper from his life." While it was the standard response to our annual gesture, it was clear he'd been touched. I guessed this was their first child.

I continued on, giving blessings and gifts to each sandling or family I came to. They blessed me far more than I blessed them; of this, I was sure. The sun was setting by the time we finished, and while I was exhausted, it was a good weariness. My siblings looked to be equally spent, but also fulfilled by the gesture judging by their smiles. Yes, new life, both immortal and mortal, it held so much promise.

I glanced about. Now to find Father and Mother. I didn't immediately see them among the throng so I asked the servant who had been assisting me, "Have you seen the king?"

"Oh, yes, Princess. He and your mother left a while back, just after we started distributing gifts."

I sighed. My heart felt like it was shrinking.

Chapter Four

I gasped, drawing a hand over my mouth where I sat on my bed. No, he couldn't mean it. Shred my wings, no.

I'd just begun to examine Kovis's thoughts as he slept, but a particularly jarring memory from the sun played over and over, so at odds with his usual, predictable, childhood thoughts of late.

Usual. Predictable. It was how things had become, despite their rocky start with the emperor accusing the twins of being murderers. Kovis and his brother had suckled, were weaned, and life had taken on a regular cadence, not much different than my previous charges, over the next seven annums.

So this... I shook my head and my stomach crawled into my throat.

> *"Enough is enough!" Emperor Altairn looked up from his report, then brought his fist down hard on the table making dishes rattle and Kovis jump where he sat, eyes wide, to the left of his father who loomed over the head. Rasa sat rod straight, not moving a muscle, to their father's right; Kennan held his breath beside her. "The peaceful sorcerers of*

Elementis have endured enough attacks from the insorcelled nations surrounding us. It's time we declare war on the nonmagical, and create a ring of territories to insulate us. They are presently unfriendly, but we will help them see the light." He nodded sharply. "It is the only way we will enjoy the lasting peace and prosperity we deserve."

Kovis was too young to understand the meaning. But I did. If the emperor carried out his plans, war would again visit us… and I knew all too well what that meant.

Like Kovis, the first time I'd experienced war I hadn't had a clue what all the talk had really meant. But it hadn't taken long for me to learn and it sent chills up my back even now.

I remembered when I'd first heard of war. All thirteen of us maidens had been in the sitting room working on our sewing projects—Mema required it, I chafed at it—and Velma, the eldest, drilled us in our history lessons while we sewed.

Velma said, "Wake realm dictates the structure of Dream realm. Put another way, each nation in Wake realm has a corresponding Dream nation. So what does that mean for sand beings?"

I'd raised my hand. "It means we shepherd the sleep and dreams of every human in that reciprocal Wake nation."

Velma bobbed her head. "That's right, Ali. Very good."

I'd smiled beside Deor. She was sharp, valued knowledge, and always encouraged me to learn.

Velma rolled her shoulders. "If you remember, Father and Grandfather designed it such that the regents they appointed when they retired, one per Dream province, ensure humans receive quality sleep and dreaming."

She blew out a long breath and I glanced over at her.

"Problem is, over time, the citizens of those provinces have started seeing their regent, rather than Father, as their sovereign. And because Father doesn't control any Dream provinces anymore, he can't do anything about it. Not without creating significant chaos in Dream."

I'd overheard Father grousing about it—he hadn't foreseen it, calling it "a strategic error" and complaining that the regents had abided by the letter of their promise, but not the spirit thereof, or some such thing. I'd never paid it much mind.

"When is the only time Dream territory can change control?" Velma asked.

Wynnfrith, my roommate, raised her hand. "Only when one Wake nation is conquered by another. It's the only time the Dream province of the winner can add it to their territory."

"Correct," Velma said, rubbing the back of her neck. She clutched the blanket she sewed.

I furrowed my brow.

"King Altairn"—her dream charge and king of the Wake nation of Water—"has designs to consolidate the seven magical nations of Wake—Water, Ice, Air, Terra, Wood, Metal, and Fire into one, calling it Elementis. I believe Father has gotten wind of it and has plans to rectify things for himself." Her voice shook.

Rectify things? My sisters gasped. Mema frowned.

I'd since learned what 'rectifying things' meant and my stomach twisted. The bloodshed required... because Father had done exactly what Velma feared.

It didn't matter that Dream regents had stopped him before he could take all of the Dream territory freed up by Wake's conquests. Didn't matter that Father had been more pissed than I'd ever seen, because of it.

What mattered was that much blood had been spilled. And it had all started when Wake's sovereign thought to improve their lot.

Kovis had no idea.

I hugged myself tight and jiggled my foot. Emperor Altairn planned to conquer the nations surrounding Elementis, as a protective barrier. I didn't fault him. Sorcerers, my dream charges, deserved to enjoy lasting peace and prosperity. But he didn't understand that his actions bore bigger consequences.

Father had been stopped the last time, and I had no doubt he would again try to retake any reciprocal Dream territories. Soldiers would suffer injury and loss in both Wake and Dream.

The thought made my stomach churn.

War was again upon us. The last one had dragged on and on over ten long annums. Would this one be over before Kovis and his siblings were old enough to fight? How I prayed so.

Chapter Five

Kovis's heart raced.

His father had headed off to war this sun and would face grave danger in his quest to conquer insorcelled barbarians. He grimaced in his sleep and a moan escaped him.

My heart ached for him. I knew firsthand the angst of being separated from my father when he'd headed off to war. Who knew if he might come to harm, or worse. My stomach twisted. The anguish of memories like that never faded. At least it hadn't for me. No doubt I'd have to endure it again, soon enough. Too soon.

I watched the gray images of Kovis's thoughts—the memory he nursed from this sun—in more detail, as he slept.

The air still held a chill, but it wasn't nippy. It wouldn't be long until the trees budded. So went Kovis's eight-annum-old thoughts, trying to distract himself as the sun rose in the sky. He took a deep breath and let it out slowly.

The sound of shod hooves on cobblestones rose as a column of men, women, and horses—a mere fraction of their forces—circled up in the lower courtyard, below. He loosed the top button on his overcoat and forced his anxious legs to still.

Rasa clenched her jaw beside him and re-smoothed the white fabric of her coat sleeve. Kennan ran a jerky hand through his brown locks, receiving a stern look from their nannies.

A supply wagon pulled by a team of four horses, creaked as it lumbered into the courtyard and stopped.

Troops uniformed in leathers accented in waist-length royal blue capes glanced up periodically and nodded as they scurried about.

Kovis shifted as his feet began to ache in his shining leather shoes. Organizing seemingly took forever, but he'd endure for it meant Father was still here, safe.

"Very good." Emperor Altairn's voice reverberated across the courtyard as his tall, muscular frame came into view, wending through those assembled.

A stable hand walked the emperor's black stallion to within a man's height and held him there.

"Mount up." The command came from an officer not far away.

As the emperor patted his mount and reached to take the reins, an officer approached and gestured, pointing. He followed the man's hand and glanced up, catching Rasa's eye—she forced a smile. Father turned and strode toward the steps leading to their roost.

He thrust the fabric of his ankle-length, royal blue cape over a leather-pauldroned shoulder as he made his way to where they stood, stopping several steps away.

"Rasa." He motioned her forward and reached out to embrace her, turning his back to the boys. Kovis couldn't hear the sentiments he expressed but when she turned, Rasa ran a quick finger under her eyes as she stepped back beside Kovis.

Kovis's heart raced and he licked his lips.

"Kovis, Kennan." Father nodded them forward.

Kovis's cheek dug into the jointures of the stiff leather but he paid no mind as his fingers clutched the soft, abundant fabric of Father's cape.

"Mind your studies while I'm gone." He patted the pair on the back, then stepped back. A stern nod sent them back into line beside their sister.

Kovis's chest tightened and his stomach clenched as his father turned and strode back down the steps, cape flying behind him.

The emperor mounted his stallion and motioned his troops forward with the wave of his hand. He never looked back.

Kovis's body felt heavy as he trudged back inside. Neither Rasa nor Kennan said anything.

I sighed. Poor Kovis. Despite the brush-off, he troubled over what might happen to his father.

I longed to suggest some action he might take that would help him feel useful, but my mind proved a blank. I shook my head and frowned. There was no remedy for worry of this sort. I knew that all too well.

Chapter Six

The sun was just setting as I flew in formation behind Deor, between Wasila and Farfelee, like I always did. It was my turn to see my father off to war. Everyone looked ahead, squinting into the sun's lengthening rays, somber and quiet.

Despite the gravity of the occasion, Mother hadn't joined us. I sighed.

A chill crawled up my spine and I cinched the buckle of my leather jacket tighter about my waist. While the ground temperature at the palace of sandmaidens had been balmy, chill winds bit into me as we flew over the rocky valleys and hills.

I beat my wings in unison with my siblings. Sand City wouldn't be much farther.

Not long after, flickering lights erupted from the dusky horizon, stretching farther than I could see.

"City Center straight ahead," Grandfather called out from where he flew beside Mema.

Shouts, whistles, and clapping grew louder as we neared the square that was the city's heart. A battalion of Father's forces looked fierce as they stood lined up in the middle—black hair and wings, bright-red capes, a gold shield affixed to their backs.

Other troops held cheering subjects back to the dirt streets surrounding the square. The crowd spotted us and their volume increased as we set down. Our guards spread out, forming a protective barrier between us and the crowds.

Father strode over. His eyes were bright and his smile broad.

My stomach went hard but I hurried to meet him anyway. I plastered on a smile, trying to push away my angst. Trying to be strong, like he expected.

"Alissandra." I hugged him tight, taking comfort in the feel of the luxurious fabric of his cape as he drew me close. I inhaled the scent of his leathers mixed with sweat. His scent.

He moved to step back but I clung to him and a chuckle rumbled through his chest. He drew a hand to my cheek and looked into my eyes. "Alissandra, I *will* return. Don't you fret."

I bobbed my head, sniffing. "I love you Father."

He grinned. "And I love you. But I need to do this. You understand don't you? Every province needs to acknowledge me..." He patted his chest. "... not some regent, as their sovereign."

I swallowed, hard and forced my head to nod.

He winked. "Now chin up."

I wiped my cheeks as I stepped back.

I blew out a breath. I'd been through this before, why was it *so* hard to say goodbye?

Kovis understood. I welcomed the rogue thought. He did. He understood what it felt like—how it hurt, anguished, grieved a body—to not know how your father fared. For eons. He'd endured it for the last nine moons, so far.

Velma put an arm around me when I reached her.

Father said his goodbyes to Grandfather, Mema, and the rest of my siblings, then strode to the front of his troops. "It is an honor leading you into battle. Now let's take some territory."

A loud cry rose from the ranks as his soldiers raised fists to the sky.

The crowds pressed in on us, their shouts and celebrations growing more frantic as Father brought his magnificent, onyx wings down and rose into the black sky.

Mema's eyes darted about, scanning the boisterous crowds, but Grandfather drew her close with an arm.

My stomach crawled into my throat as bright-red capes fluttered in the rush of air and the host rose above the shops, up, up, and up, quickly disappearing into the night sky.

"Let's go home," Grandfather said, without enthusiasm.

War was again upon us. There was no denying it.

My only solace, my dream charge understood what I felt, deeply, intimately. We'd endure this together.

Chapter Seven

My stomach quivered. What would I find as I watched Kovis's thoughts as he slept?

Our fathers were both still off at war. I bit my lip as I settled my wings behind the headboard and sank down on the bed.

Nestling into the abundant pillows, I reached out to Kovis and found his thought thread. But it seemed to wave more erratically than usual, as if desperate for my attentions, for relief I might offer to his tumultuous thoughts. I took a deep breath and plunged in.

Dressed in his royal-blue robe with the collar of his white pajamas showing, Kovis wound his way ahead of his similarly clad siblings, through the abundant flowers, trees, and other foliage, past the gazebo, on paths that meandered about the empress's garden.

"Here," Rasa said, stopping near a fountain that burbled in the dark.

Kennan thrust out the blanket he'd carried folded under his arm and the trio spread it out, then sat.

Kovis lay back and took in the rainbow of colors that hung like a curtain rippling in a gentle breeze in the night sky—greens and purples and reds and turquoise and yellows and blues against the black. The stars painted a breathtaking backdrop to the display.

Kennan picked a blade of ground cover and began sucking on it.

Rasa exhaled loudly. "I don't think I'll ever get tired of watching the Lights."

They fell silent for some time.

"I love the crackling sound that the Canyon's energy makes." Kovis said, breaking the quiet. "That power will flow through our veins one sun. When my powers manifest, I'm going to be a powerful fire mage. Fire and Air. I'll create infernos. It'll be awesome."

"I thought you wanted to wield Fire and Water, like Father" Rasa questioned.

"I did but I decided I want to use my powers together, not one at a time. Imagine two powers that enhance each other." His eyes shone.

Kennan laughed. "That would be amazing. I still want to be an Ice mage. They can make such amazing sculptures."

"Always the artist," Kovis said, smiling.

"What's wrong with that?"

"Nothing. Nothing at all."

"Well, I don't really care which magic I have. I'll be empress. And when I am, I'm going to make sure that mages and nonmagical people get along."

"Well aren't you the wise ruler." Kovis chuckled.

"What? You don't think magical and insorcelled people can get along?" Rasa frowned.

Kovis gave her a long look. "It would beat going to war." It came out a whisper and he shuffled his feet.

Rasa's face took on a grave expression and Kennan's shoulders slumped.

● ● ●

"Seriously though," Kovis added, several heartbeats later. "I think you'll make a good ruler and get them all to cooperate."

"Thanks for the vote of confidence." Rasa held her lips in a line.

"And I'll help you." Kovis smiled.

"Me too," Kennan added.

Rasa reached over and took Kovis's, then Kennan's hand and gently squeezed.

The trio fell silent as the crackling Lights again grabbed their attention.

How long they watched the skies in wonder I didn't count, but I exhaled. Unlike his usual thoughts of late, these were dreams I loved to weave. Kovis had so much potential and fostering his vision of the future excited me.

My limbs felt lighter than they had in ages.

Kovis would be an absolutely amazing sorcerer, I had no doubt. Call me biased, but every one of my charges was special. And he was mine... My heart warmed.

Kovis was my eighth charge, and while I had loved each and every one of the seven before him, I hadn't felt about them like I did him. No, I felt a special connection with Kovis.

Kovis may have only been nine, but he and I understood each other. I'd never get to meet him, not in person at least, but if I did, I knew we'd click. There was something about going through Hades itself, feeling bone-wearying angst over not knowing the whereabouts or well-being of your father that bound beings together.

And his mother had... I hated the word 'abandoned.' I resisted using it. But she'd abandoned him... like Mother had, us. Whether Kovis's mother's separation was voluntarily or not—neither Alfreda nor I had hazarded a guess—the result was the same.

Before Kovis, I hadn't begun to understand unfulfilled longing. As yet, I claimed no competence, but I at least had another to commiserate with.

These and other similar notions washed over me and I soaked them in. Feeling understood and deeply connected, was a balm to my very soul. I hoped I could be and do for Kovis, what he'd unknowingly done for me.

But my stomach clenched as his thoughts came into focus.

Chapter Eight

I was determined to create a happy dream for Kovis tonight. By the
Ancient One, he surely deserved one. I'd nearly cried last night as I
tried to ease his lingering pain.

The weather had been warmer than usual, the snows had
melted, and Emperor Altairn left, returning to the front early, a
sennight before Kovis's and his twin's tenth birthday—seven
stinking suns. His quest was *that* important?

I gnashed my teeth. I had a few choice words for that... man. Too
bad I'd never have opportunity to tell him to his face.

I breathed deeply, trying to loose my frustration, as I took hold
of Kovis's thought thread and let his thoughts unfold.

> *"Excuse me, Master Readingham," Kovis said, as he*
> *entered a room with weapons of all sorts standing against,*
> *and hanging from, its walls. Sorcerers sat polishing arms,*
> *but halted and went down on one knee at seeing him.*
>
> *The sound of hammering rippled from a doorway not*
> *far off.*

"Why, Prince Kovis, what can I do for you?" The coltish man turned and bowed, as well. His leathers made no sound—a clear sign of their abundant use.

"I just turned ten. You said as soon as I did, you'd start training me with weapons." Determination filled Kovis's eyes.

"So I did, my prince." Readingham smiled. "Is Prince Kennan also seeking instruction?"

"No, Master."

The man gave an assessing nodded. "Very well. Then let's have Faramond get you properly suited up, and we'll start you with some instruction on wielding a dagger."

"Thank you, Master."

Kovis's excitement made his heart race even now.

My breathing caught. Was he doing this to earn his father's favor? The timing seemed more than coincidence. Were we the same, even in this? I hated admitting it, even to myself, but deep down I knew it to be true.

Kovis had figured it out, too. And I would support him in his quest. He deserved to know his father's love. We both did.

———————————

The war raged on and on and on, but Kovis's determination never flagged. He nursed thoughts of this morning as he slept.

Kovis lingered at breakfast.

Father nursed a fresh cup of coffee, seated at the head of the table in this, the smaller, private dining room.

The door snit shut behind the steward as he left. The timer—Father finishing his coffee—started.

No one would be interrupting them—Kennan had left to attend to his studies. Rasa hadn't appeared. Again. As had become her habit. Tenseness filled Kovis's stomach but he pushed it aside and drew his napkin across his mouth.

He straightened and cleared his throat. "Father."

The emperor's eyes moved from the stack of reports he'd been digesting and focused on his son, taking a sip.

"Master Readingham has been instructing me over the last two annums." Kovis leashed his emotions and despite being excited, his voice remained even.

"Has he now?"

Kovis felt his father's eyes roam over him, sizing him up, but he continued. "He's been showing me how to fight with a dagger. May I show you what I can do before you return to the front?"

A smile emerged on the emperor's face. "Well, my boy, you might actually make something useful of yourself."

"Thank you, Father." Kovis beamed as a lightness filled his chest.

Joy filled my heart. We both longed for a relationship with our fathers, to have their respect.

I exhaled. Yes, that was a part, but really, we both just wanted to be loved, unconditionally.

Kovis viewed this as progress and I agreed. Anything I could do to encourage him on his way, I'd do. I clenched my fist. We'd realize our desires if it was the last thing we did, both of us.

My stomach tightened. But what lengths would we be forced to go to, to succeed?

Chapter Nine

"It seems the regents of the territories your father has not yet reclaimed—Naverey, Anarit, and Abuj—have banded together despite their differences and stopped his campaign," Mema announced over dinner this morn.

My hand froze, a fork full of rangoon halfway to my mouth. Stopped him? He'd been thwarted on his first campaign. But again? Oh, he'd be pissed.

"He'll be home within a moon."

My eyes lit up, and I set my fork down. The war in Dream was over—no more killing and bloodshed. Father was coming home. He'd be mad, but he'd be home, nonetheless. I drew my hands to my chest.

Farfelee seemed equally excited judging by the twinkle that crept into her eyes. Alfreda clapped quietly, across from me.

Velma sighed, loudly.

I furrowed my brow and looked down the table at her. Clearly, I'd missed something. What was I not understanding?

I still hadn't sorted out what I'd missed as the prolific, squat sand homes of Sand City came into view suns later. Grandfather, Mema, my siblings and I soared over the hills bordering the city as the sun's lengthening rays warmed and drove off some of the chill in the evening air, but I still shivered.

Hoots and hollers from citizens lining the square at the heart of City Center rose to welcome us as we followed Rowntree and Baldik, two of our family's guards, setting down on the empty dirt-covered space. Our other ten guards encircled us, jaws clenched, eyes roaming the pressing crowd.

"This way," Baldik said, extending an arm. "We'd like you to wait in The Salty Seahorse, for your own safety."

Rowntree mimicked the gesture, directing us toward our favorite tavern, one of the fine establishments lining the square. He and Rowntree were the largest guards in the palace and usually lead our security detail whenever we ventured out. Their thumbs twitched above the swords at their sides.

I'd never been in the tavern as the sun set, hadn't ever thought to, as it was closed at this point of every sun. But the hinges of the worn, wooden door squeaked in greeting when another of our guards pushed it open.

Barnabas, the establishment's gray-headed, round-bellied proprietor's eyes lit as he scurried from behind the bar. "Welcome, welcome. So glad to see you all again. Please, come in, come in." The long tuft of hair he'd combed over his balding head, flew up as he waved a weathered hand over the dozen empty, well-worn tables scattered about the dimly lit space.

The ceiling that I guessed had originally been white stucco was gray from the smoke of the army of lanterns it took to illuminate it, what with only a few, small windows in the front and back. Cobwebs hung from the muscular wooden trusses, swaying in the drafts.

We spread out, filling the cozy place. I seated myself in one of the wobbly chairs at a small table. Harding joined me to my right. The sound of chair legs scrapping across well-worn floorboards rose as Clovis, my baby brother, and Alfreda scooted their chairs in to fill out our group.

I grinned as I looked Clovis over. "Nice hair, little brother."

"Thank you." He puffed out his chest.

As always, he'd sculpted his black hair with Dyeus only knew how much hair stiffener to mark the occasion we commemorated. This sun it held the shape of a winged sandal. I shook my head. It was an unabashed, original style, just like him. I wondered what he'd come up with next.

Edeva, Barnabas's full-figured wife, beamed as she wiped her hands on her apron. "You must be so happy to see the king again," she said, stopping beside me.

"I am. We are." I ruffled my wings.

My siblings bobbed their heads in agreement.

A corner of her mouth turned up when she spotted Clovis, but she stifled a grin and asked, "So what breakfast can we scramble up for you?"

"How's Breena?" I asked Harding once Edeva left.

Breena was his current dream charge, a juvenile Air sorceress, studying at the capital in Veritas. She was head over heels after a sorcerer boy, some councilman's son, who wielded Fire and Water magical powers.

He smirked.

Clovis raised his brows. Alfreda leaned in.

A smile mounted my face as I rested my chin on my folded hands.

"If you remember, Breena is rather peculiar and particular about her fashion."

"Oh, yes." I sniggered. I'd never forget Harding's earlier tales of the girl's wardrobe proclivities—lots and lots of feathers, dangly beads, jewelry made in part with dead insects, chicken leather accessories, hair-covered rings, shed-snake skin sashes. The list went on and on and agonizingly on.

"Well, apparently Liam decided to show off what he's been learning about harnessing his talents." Harding snorted and slapped the table.

Mema glanced over with a stern look from where she and Grandfather sat sipping coffee, two tables down.

"Breena had gotten all spiffy-ed up in a new dress. She'd spent way too long arranging her hair, painting her nails, the works." My sibling rolled his eyes. "Anyway, the lad brought her to a lovely overlook, a rise with a view of the capital. He proceeded to ignite a flame above his head then conjure some sort of cloud above it." Harding took a sip of coffee Edeva had delivered. "It was pretty impressive seeing the water and flames comingle, then expunge themselves all while he kept feeding it power."

"But…" I interjected, jiggling a foot.

"Yes, but." Harding smiled. "Liam told Breena to step beside him, promised her he'd keep her safe and dry."

"And…" Alfreda bit her lip, eyes wide.

"And she did."

"Okay…" Clovis motioned to speed up the telling.

"He leaned over and planted a searing kiss on her lips. All while keeping his magic going."

"Oop. What a male." I thumped the table.

The rest of my siblings, all eighteen of them, plus Mema and Grandfather turned their heads toward us.

Harding held up his hand. "But there's more. Breena was so surprised that her Air magic erupted and she knocked Liam's balance off."

I sucked in a breath.

Harding laughed. "Liam snuffed out his flame in time, but Breena's new dress, coiffed hair, painted nails, all of it, got absolutely drenched."

Alfreda and my mouths dropped open.

"But instead of being steamed about it, she grabbed the boy by the shoulders and brought her lips crashing down on his."

"Aw…" I sighed. "Young love."

Edeva stopped beside us with a tray crammed with our selections.

"Speaking of love…" Clovis said, wagging his brows at me, after our hostess left.

Alfreda drew her hand up quickly, hiding a mouthful of food as well as a smirk.

"Alfreda's been telling me a thing or two about you and your charge, Prince Kovis isn't it?"

I scowled at my sister. Little rat.

Unrepentant, she snickered.

I took a bite of my dreamberry muffin, trying to hide a smile. Long ago, they'd wheedled out of me my obsession with Kovis's royal blue eyes with hazel centers. Bless the Ancient One, I'd never seen eyes like his—not on any of my charges. I wished I was able to see them more, but alas, only when I wove dreams from his memories of seeing himself in a mirror. I'd first spotted them when he was but a babe.

So what, that the images still floated through my head. On and off. With more regularity the older he'd grown.

I cleared my throat. "What about me and my charge?"

"Seems he and his twin have begun maturing, physically." He grinned.

"And…" I tamped down on the sudden warmth that beset my cheeks.

"Seems he's got a little acne, and his voice has taken on a bit of a squeak of late, a squeak that you seem to think is… and I quote, 'the cutest thing you've ever heard.'"

I glared at Alfreda, but couldn't quell my traitorous cheeks. I drew my hands up and my siblings burst out laughing.

Dyeus help me.

"They're here." Baldik announced, standing in the open door.

I exhaled. Thank the Ancient One.

Harding winked. Clovis grinned.

I wagged a finger in Alfreda's face as we rose. She just sniggered.

More subjects had jammed the square, and they were waving, clapping, and cheering as we made it outside and through the throng to the empty square.

I looked up into the dark sky and caught sight of Father at the head of his troops which flew in formation. As one, they swooped down and landed in the square.

And the crowds went wild.

I concentrated, trying to make out what Father said over the noise. "It has been an honor leading you. You are dismissed." Short and sweet. Father's shoulders slumped for a heartbeat before he corrected and saluted his ranks.

What had been leathers with bright red capes and gleaming gold shields outfitting these soldiers, were now battle worn and torn. Some troops no longer had shields. Gray had replaced the red on their capes. They'd faced some serious fighting.

My stomach clenched. How many wouldn't be returning. The wounded were probably coming with the horse-drawn supply wagons several sennights from now.

Father strode toward us, grim faced.

For the first time, I didn't race to meet him. I'd known he wouldn't take kindly to being stopped.

Mema and Grandfather exchanged idle chatter with him until he cut them off, saying, "Let's just go home."

He was pissed, no doubt about it. His expectations had gone unfulfilled. Again. It would haunt him. I could see it in his eyes.

I drew a hand to my chest as my stomach grew hard.

He'd try to reengage the battle at some point. It wouldn't be right away, but he would. This was far from over for Father.

Chapter Ten

The war was over in Dream, but it raged on in Wake. Happy heartbeats were few and far between. I bit my lip as I found Kovis's thought thread. What had happened this sun? What would I have to help him work through? I exhaled and plunged in.

"In here." Kovis wrenched the door handle open and, still grasping Amice's hand, he pulled her through into the dark guest room. The music from the ball going on one floor below filtered up and lent a sophisticated air to what he hoped would happen.

"Wait right here," Kovis said. The sound of clinking glass and a drawer sliding open echoed in the quiet a heartbeat later.

"What are you doing, my prince?" The voice of the councilman's daughter hitched.

"There we go." Amice came into view as Kovis lit the beeswax candle, then dropped the globe back down to protect the flame. He repeated with four more candles before turning.

His smile wavered as he retraced his steps, taking in her strapless sapphire gown. Candlelight caught the clear beads and made them look like tiny flames igniting her bodice and trailing down her skirts.

"You're sure no one will...." Amice rubbed her arms.

"Let me lock the door."

The maiden bit her lip as she nodded.

Kovis's hands had turned sweaty, and he brushed them against his tunic before returning and extending them. "If you don't want to, we don't have to..."

"No, I want to." Insistence filled her voice. "It's just I've never... you know. Have you?"

Kovis cleared his throat. "Of... of course."

He led Amice to the divan and, with an open palm, invited her to sit, then took a seat beside.

"You're sure they won't miss us?" She fidgeted with her hands.

"I told my father I was going to get some fresh air in Mother's garden. You told your parents the same. They'll be too busy impressing each other to notice. I hate balls."

Amice tittered. "But if it weren't for the lightning dance, we couldn't..."

Kovis smiled. "You make a fair point, maiden. So... shall we...?" His hand trembled as he brushed the back of it against Amice's jaw.

She reached up, captured it in hers, then drew it to her lips.

Kovis's groin throbbed, but he tried to ignore as he leaned forward and lightly pressed his lips to hers, then pulled back.

Amice smiled, "I liked that."

"Do... do you want to do it again?" Kovis asked.

Her eyes danced as she leaned closer, then found his lips. She wanted him, he knew it. Was this what love was supposed to look like? The thought thundered across his mind as Amice pressed the kiss further.

● ● ●

Several heartbeats later Kovis pulled back, but brought a hand to the back of her neck and began stroking it with his thumb. "You're very beautiful."

Amice looked down. "Thank you. Mother tells me I'll sweep men off their feet, but between you and me, I think she and Father just see me as an opportunity to advance their status. Marry me off to the right prospect, and they'll look even better."

Kovis's mind whirled. How do I show her I care without possessing her? What will she think if I rub her shoulder? But not like Father. Kovis's stomach clenched. "That's too bad, but I know the feeling. My powers haven't yet manifested. I know I'm late at fifteen, but because of it, Father believes I'll be powerful. He's got designs for me to help him win the war, he's said as much." He sighed before continuing, "Imagine if they knew we were..."

They shared a chuckle.

Kovis pulled his hand back, but his ring snagged a lock of her long caramel hair. "Oh." Kovis fumbled, not wanting to hurt her.

Amice reached up and grabbed her hair above the tangle. "My prince, stop." Amice brought her other hand up and stilled his. "Slide your ring off."

Using his other hand to steady the ring, Kovis twisted back and forth several times until it slipped off.

"I bet you haven't had that happen when you're... getting intimate with a girl," Amice joked.

"No... no, you're right. I haven't." Kovis's mouth opened and closed like a fish, wanting, but daring not to offer advice as he watched her work to free her hair from his ring. She finally succeeded and handed it back to him.

Putting the ring on, he looked up and chuckled. "I've made a mess of things haven't I?"

A corner of Amice's mouth turned up. "It's nice to see the crown prince is human. So what were you going to do before that happened?"

Kovis looked down. "I was going to rub your shoulder."

Amice drew a hand to her hair and tossed it behind her.

She still wanted to... "Removing it from danger?" Kovis tried to quip but it came out strained.

"Something like that."

Kovis pushed back jitters as he brought his fingers to her shoulder and began circling them. *What does uncorrupted affection look like?* Kovis pondered. *What would she like?*

Several heartbeats later, he let his hand drop and traced the top of her dress with a finger. She watched his every move but he sensed curiosity, not fear or worry like with Rasa, the times he'd rescued her.

She looked up and met his eyes, "Go ahead."

"Are... are you sure?" Kovis swallowed as Amice nodded.

She wanted this. He definitely wanted this, and his groin left no doubt. He reached into her bodice, cupped her breast, and drew it up.

"It's so soft, so round." It came out a murmur.

"I thought you'd been intimate before." Amice giggled.

Kovis didn't respond with the whole of his focus on the treasure he held. He took to stroking it with his other hand.

"Do you like me doing this?"

"Mmm, yes." Amice freed her other breast from the dress and Kovis divided his attention between the pair.

"Lie back," Kovis said as he slipped to the floor and knelt beside her. He surrendered to the urges that seemed to flow like blood through his veins, kissing her breasts, then suckling them, then licking their pink tips.

Amice moaned with pleasure through it all. Kovis added his own notes of pleasure and soon a high pitched "Oh... oh... oh..." harmonized with his sounds.

● ● ●
54

Kovis pulled back and studied her face, her closed eyes, her wrinkled brow, unsure what to do. Was he hurting her?

"Don't. Stop," she pleaded as she bucked her hips.

Kovis licked a pink nipple and sucked.

A soft sound of pleasure escaped her lips in response.

She was enjoying this. He was bringing her pleasure. He opened his mouth wide and filled it with her other breast, then made circles with his tongue around her pebbled tip. He could pleasure a woman. Intimacy that both people sought was possible.

His groin pained him and the buttons of his breeches strained as she stilled, but her face had taken on the most serene look.

"That was amazing. Mmm," Amice murmured several heartbeats later.

The doorknob jiggled. "Brother, are you in there?" Knocking further interrupted the quiet, and Amice shot up, hiding her breasts, and smoothing her skirts.

Kovis looked to the ceiling and rolled his eyes.

I grinned, no doubt happier than the experience demanded as relief flooded me. The war had been the last of Kovis's worries. And what's more, his first sexual encounter had been positive, such a contrast to... I shook my head. No, I would not corrupt this... with *that.*

He was fifteen and I should have seen the signs. It shouldn't have been a surprise, but it had been all the same. Kovis was no different than my previous male charges in this respect. Healthy. He was a healthy male.

I growled. If only his siblings enjoyed the same healthiness...

Chapter Eleven

Time passed, but that bloody war dragged on and on in Wake. Kovis and I were both sick to death of it. At least his father was home from the front for the winter. But I about pulled my hair out as I watched Kovis's thoughts as he slept.

"Damn you!" Emperor Altairn roared. "Your sister manifested at thirteen and Kennan at fourteen. You're sixteen and still can't so much as attempt a spark of magic." A flame danced between the man's fingers.

Kovis bit his tongue, barely holding his temper in check where he stood, bare-chested despite the winter chill, in one of the ovals sorcerers trained in. He swiped the back of his arm across his brow.

Clenching his jaw, the tall, muscular man strode over to Kovis. "Perhaps you inherited your mother's magic..." Under his breath he added, "... make you a timid healer on the battlefield. I'm sure the enemy would love that." His father sent him a piercing glare.

Kovis's heart raced but he remained silent in the man's shadow. He'd worked so hard to win his father's favor. He'd already risen to be one of the top swordsmen according to Master Readingham, but it was all falling apart.

Emperor Altairn swatted the air as he turned his back, looked up and bellowed, "Send him down!"

"Yes, majesty!" came a quick reply and Kennan, clad in orange, loose-fitting drawstring pants soon descended the stairs. Gooseflesh pimpled his bare arms and developing chest.

Kennan caught Kovis's eyes for a heartbeat, but glanced away just as quickly, meeting his father's.

The emperor patted Kennan's shoulder with a sinewy hand when he reached him, then nodded him to the top of the oval pit.

"Come here, Kovis." It came out a growl. "You're weak. You're not even trying."His tattooed chest glowed bright red as he brought his hands down, in one quick, frustrated motion. "Enough."

Kovis's heart picked up pace as he stopped beside his father and caught another furtive glance from his twin.

"You will stop me or your brother will suffer."

Kovis sucked in a breath. His eyes darted to Kennan, whose chest rose and fell too quickly, feet spread, bracing.

The emperor took the stance he'd instructed Kovis to assume a million times before and in a heartbeat, conjured a ball of flame in his bare hand.

Kovis exhaled. Kennan was also a fire mage. Father couldn't burn him.

The ball of fire sailed to the top of the oval and Kennan easily caught it, then snuffed it out.

Staring Kovis down, the emperor chuckled. "Think he's in no danger?"

Kovis's heart surged as a white ball of flame materialized above his head. Heat radiating off it made sweat bead his brow. His head started to sting but he dared not flinch.

"Stop me, damn it!"

Kovis studied his hands, willing them, begging them to cooperate like he'd tried so many times before. How was he to conjure magic if he had not a clue what powers of the Canyon flowed in his veins? If any even did.

Sweat droplets wet his palms.

The emperor shook his head and huffed. "Fine." In a heartbeat the molten orb flew toward the top of the oval.

Kennan shrieked.

"No!" Terror filled Kovis's feet.

"Stay! Now stop it!"

Another anguished scream.

Kovis's lungs refused air as he fumbled, focusing, trying to conjure Fire, Wood, Terra, then Metal. Anything to save Kennan. Nothing happened.

He pulled at his hair, screaming his frustration.

Another cry.

The emperor swallowed up the white orb with a thought.

Hatred and loathing filled Kovis as his chest heaved, gasping for air, bent over, hands on his knees. He finally straightened and recited, "Fire, Wood, Terra, and Metal. I tried them all, father. They didn't work. I really tried."

Kennan moaned, writhing in the sand.

The emperor frowned. "Then perhaps you should try the ones you didn't." And with that, he conjured a stream of water and directed it at the top of the oval.

Kennan wailed as water reached him, pummeling him where he lay—fire and metal, his affinities, were no contest, not against their father who was also a seasoned Water sorcerer.

The sound of blood coursing, pounding, filled Kovis's ears. It faded into a muted background as his vision

• • •

tunneled and he thrust out his hands. He had to stop Father's water.

Kennan wailed.

Air. He sought Air. Willed it's power into existence. He'd rip it from the very Canyon itself. A roar rose, filling his ears alongside the pounding.

Another cry, weaker, from his twin. His blood. They'd shared everything. Knew each other intimately. Two halves of the same beating heart. His brother. And he would save him.

"Gods! Help me!" Kovis screamed at the top of his lungs.

Father's blast met resistance. Water sprayed. Everywhere.

Except at Kennan who lay limp in a swamp of wet sand.

Water. Come to me! The thought loosed another growl that rose, becoming a roar and Kovis threw his fisted hands into the air releasing a torrent. Anger. Rage. Fury. He turned the deluge back on his tormentor, holding nothing back.

The emperor laughed as he blended with the onslaught.

Ice. The thought sent a wave of glee through Kovis and his father's crazed laughter muted as a coat of thick, solid, unyielding freeze blanketed him. Layer upon layer upon layer. Kovis's ire-given-substance, pelted, coated, sealed away his foe. More. More. More.

"The emperor!" Shouts rose from onlookers.

Ice mages, three of them, neutralized Kovis's onslaught as they directed their power down, into the pit, from where they braced around the top of the oval.

More anger. More rage. Kovis redoubled his retribution, pummeling the ice-coated man with more and more and more water. The fifth Water mage finally blunted the deluge.

Enmity, exasperation, hatred fueled him further and he turned his attention back to his winds, buffeting his still frozen father.

His feet left the ground and he flipped then slammed into a hard wall of Air, before thudding to the sand.

Grains filled his mouth and nose. He choked then coughed, returning to his senses. Four Air mages locked eyes on him, unmoving, open palms directed at him, holding him down.

"Release," one of the Air mages commanded.

Kovis spit and nodded, panting.

A hush blanketed the pit.

Until Kennan moaned.

My nostrils flared. I ground my teeth. I'd always hated Emperor Altairn but this... I wanted to scream. This went beyond the pale. The man was a menace, pure and simple.

He didn't deserve Kovis.

I panted, trying to harness my fury.

His sandmaiden. I shook my head. Poor Delcina. Daughter of a commoner, picked out of obscurity, and thrust into the limelight because Father had taken a liking to her. I'd felt sorry for her before, but more so now, having to deal with Emperor Altairn—King Altairn, his ancestor, hadn't been nearly so disagreeable, at least Velma had never complained about him as she wove his dreams. But Delcina deserved a medal for putting up with this human. Had I been her, I questioned whether I would grant him sleep and weave his dreams. It would serve him right to go without for a time.

With Kovis's powers manifesting, dread filled me. It felt as if I waited for the other shoe to drop as I watched his thoughts each night. I knew what would happen. It had with another of my charges during the first war.

Sure enough, my worst fears were recognized not long after as Emperor Altairn prepared to return to the front with the spring thaw.

"Your powers have manifested. You're expected to fight."

The emperor looked Kovis up and down.

Kovis remained silent.

"More importantly, you're a prince of the realm. It's time you lived up to your responsibilities." The man picked up his coffee and took a sip.

Kovis's thoughts were a whirl as he chewed.

"Your siblings and I will return to the front next moon. You will accompany us." Under his breath he added, "About time."

"Thank you, Father." Kovis wiped his mouth and laid the napkin on his plate.

Kovis was only sixteen. Sixteen. And untrained. How I abhorred the man. How *did* Delcina endure him? Never had I had such an objectionable charge. I huffed.

Turning my thoughts to Kovis, I took another breath and let it out slowly, then began weaving: You're young, yes. But you're powerful. So, so, powerful, Kovis. And your father knows it.

I paused. The fact that the emperor required Kovis to go, had to mean he'd made progress in earning the man's respect. And respect was a stepping stone to love, right? I sighed. Why was gaining a father's love so hard?

I shook the heartache Kovis and I knew all too well away and continued weaving: *Your father respects you...* in his own way. He would not have... invited... you if he hadn't been confident you could handle yourself in combat. You're untrained, but you saved Kennan—and he'll be there, too. So will Rasa. You're strong. You can face your worst fears and overcome them.

This and more I wove into his dreams this night, convincing myself as much as he.

———————

The next two annums dragged by as each night I counted down the heartbeats until it would be time for Kovis to sleep and I could rejoin his thoughts. Worry that I might not find him or his thought thread ate at me. Anxiety plagued me. I couldn't eat. And I kept biting my sister's heads off.

How I abhorred war.

So I exhaled, relief filling me, as I found him tonight. I held my breath as I watched the memory he nursed.

> *Kovis beamed and chest bumped his brothers in arms. "Two annums. Two, long, bloody annums I've been fighting."*
>
> *"Woohoo!" Kennan crowed from beside him, seated on a makeshift stool, inside the threadbare tent the ten sorcerers shared.*
>
> *"I've been fighting for five," Ogier said, shaking his head. "It's finally over."*
>
> *"Five? I've been at this for ten. Since the very beginning." Milo tossed back a shot of amber liquid.*
>
> *"I still can't believe it. The emperor brokered a deal with Juba," Herbert, cheek scarred from an enemy dagger, rose and patted Kovis's shoulder.*
>
> *"The last insorcelled territory to fall." Tobias rubbed his brow.*
>
> *"Woo!" Kennan yelled again.*
>
> *"What are you going to do now?" Ogier threw the question out.*
>
> *Conversation and celebration continued long into the night.*

Joy filled me. I doubted my smile could grow wider. I wanted to squeal, hoot, yell.

The war was finally over. It was over. There would be no more fighting, no more loss of life in Wake. And Elementis would enjoy the protection the new territories would provide.

The rising sun pinked the sky outside our window. I jiggled my foot shaking my whole bed, waiting for Wynnfrith to finish weaving her charge's dreams. I had to share the good news, although, she probably already knew. Kovis couldn't have been the only one with celebrations on his mind.

Several heartbeats passed and I huffed quietly. Wynnfrith's eyes were still shut. She didn't look to be finishing yet, not with the pained expression she currently wore. Her charge didn't share my joy.

Kovis was safe. I settled back into the pillows and grinned. Such a momentous occasion needed to be commemorated, but how?

Grandfather had memorialized his retirement, aka The Transition, by enacting the Festival of Sandlings.

When I'd completed my apprenticeship, they'd given me a new designation, sandmaiden.

Humans put markers on the graves of loved ones who passed on.

What would I do to mark this occasion?

I smiled. Kovis made me happy. He was becoming quite the male. He'd filled out during the war, and I'd started fantasizing about running my hands over his muscled chest.

My cheeks warmed at the thought. It was a good thing I could only see him flex those muscles when his thoughts were of standing before a mirror. I snickered quietly.

I'd noticed physical changes as my previous male charges had matured, as well. I wasn't blind. But I'd never allowed myself to fantasize about them. No, those relationships had been strictly me, a sand maiden, helping her charge. But that deep connection I felt with Kovis—that common bond, knowing each other at the deepest, most intimate, most vulnerable level—had changed that. I wasn't sure when it had happened, but it had. And I didn't regret it.

My sisters would give me no end of grief if they knew.

But an idea sparked. Kovis was my dream charge, but he made me beam. Dream charge. Beam. Dream charge beam. Dream beam. Dreambeam. Dreambeam. Yes, that was it.

I'd call him my Dreambeam.

I stifled a snicker, quickly glancing at Wynnfrith—she starred back.

I sucked in a breath.

Chapter Twelve

"As you know Ali has a tendency to talk to herself. Quietly, but out loud," Wynnfrith said from her perch on the sofa in the sitting room, after this morning's fortnight family dinner.

She wouldn't spread my nonsensical ramblings. My stomach tensed with embarrassment.

"Oh, Kovis. Dreambeam." Wynnfrith raised her voice to mimic mine, probably imitating some actress in one of the plays she'd seen at the theater of late. If I hadn't loved my roommate so much, I'd have killed her.

Several of my siblings' eyes went wide. Others beamed, and chuckles rumbled through our midst.

My cheeks burned and I drew my hands to cover them.

Clovis made kissing sounds, no doubt imitating something one of his charges had done.

A corner of Alfreda's mouth turned up.

I held up my hands. "Now just wait." I cleared my throat. "Okay, I admit I like Kovis. But what's not to like, he's been a great charge."

"Uh huh," Harding said, winking.

"Just stop. It's not like that."

Smirks met my protests.

"You make it sound as if I feel about Kovis the way Father acted out his feelings about Delcina." It had been a fortnight family dinner right after Emperor Altairn declared war on the nonmagical nations surrounding Elementis.

Velma coughed as silence blanketed the room. No one would forget. Father had hosted. He'd sat in his usual seat at the head table, on a raised platform a couple of handbreadths above us in his high-ceilinged dining room.

Delcina, his latest mistress, had been situated a bit too close to him for my comfort, but I refrained from comment. Father had always been daring, but as his boredom from retirement had grown, he'd become increasingly brazen and taken to entertaining mistresses. He'd never married Mother, so clearly, he felt no conflict.

My siblings and I looked on from where we sat around four circular tables. Either Father didn't care that we saw or he wanted us to watch. With him as he was these suns, either was believable.

Father ran his fingers through Delcina's long black locks, then took his time, brushing them behind her shoulder. I tried to keep my own shoulders still as I shifted in my chair. I feared what he'd do next. This wasn't the first time he'd shown affection to a female... publicly.

Delcina's dress, while long-sleeved, had been fashioned principally of black mesh, to compliment her hair and wings. Only two narrow, black satin strips covered much of anything, falling from her shoulders to her waist. It did little to cover her olive skin. I had no doubt Father had picked it out himself. No, actually, if he'd picked it out, she would have been wearing less, if anything at all. I flexed my hands again, trying to cope.

I'd arrived after she'd been seated and was glad the tablecloth obstructed my view. I didn't want to know what the bottom half of her dress looked like. I suspected it carried the top's theme downward, no doubt giving Father quite the view of her abundant curves from beside her.

I coughed, doing anything to ignore the goings on.

● ● ●

Father started nuzzling and sucking on her neck. His excitement made his wings quiver and his fingers soon started tracing idle circles on her shoulder. I looked away and started tapping my heel, repulsed by the display. Others of my sisters looked equally uncomfortable, clenching jaws and biting lips.

Utensils brushing china were the only sounds that filled the room. Brushing... petting... my spoon clattered as I dropped it. I'd been licking the lingering cheese off. When had eating turned seductive? My siblings as well as the servers seemed equally disquieted. A collective sigh filled the room when Father finally sat back, shifting his wings. But his fingers didn't still. He continued circling Delcina's shoulder.

He took a bite of his braised vegetables and cheesy noodles, chewed, then swallowed.

I wished he choked on them. Anything to stop this.

After taking a sip of wine, he dug in to his white-pepper cloud soup. He smiled and conversed with her, as if the scene was completely normal. He winked and she blushed. Again.

While awaiting the main course, Father planted a host of claiming kisses on her lips, then started swirling that same finger at the base of her neck, on the soft innermost feathers of her wings. Delcina shivered and her wings rustled. No surprise, I would have too. It was only the most sensitive and erotic spot we had until we loosened our wings. Oh Dyeus... would he... would they?

I rubbed my arms willing Father to stop.

Dessert. They served coconut dream rolls. I couldn't help but spot the humor—the shape, the color, the notion of Father exercising a certain part of his anatomy with this female. It made my stomach... roll, in a very different way.

I glanced at my brothers. Most looked conflicted, wanting to condemn what was happening, but also struggling to be better than their base natures, which excited when seeing such things. I knew those of my brothers who examined their plates had mastered the situation, but others seemed to be losing despite it being repulsive with our father doing it. Velma and I sent chilling looks to a few.

I fidgeted and pulled my wings closer. Most of my sisters squirmed. Some tried to cover their discomfort, pushing their dessert around their plates.

Father finished his dessert, pushed back, and pulled Delcina onto his lap—my suspicions about the lower half of her dress were borne out. Father proceeded to nibble at her neck and she let her wings loosen a bit, inviting the lazy strokes that his fingers started on the feathers at the top of her back.

Velma closed her eyes.

Delcina had nearly fully unfurled her wings leaving virtually nothing to the imagination by the time dinner ended.

But ever the performer, Father finally looked up, scanned his audience, and chuckled. "You'll excuse us." It came out a purr. "We have a *pressing* engagement to attend to." And with that, he stood Delcina up. She furled her wings, and they waltzed out with her on his arm. He chuckled the whole way.

The doors clicked shut behind them. It felt as if the air itself followed them out, leaving nothing but a vacuum.

My heart raced. My blood rushed. These were the only sounds that filled my head for several heartbeats. I wasn't alone judging by the silence.

No, no one would ever forget that dinner.

My thoughts returned from the gruesome memories of that long ago dinner and I nodded sharply. "See. It's not like that with Kovis."

"I should certainly hope not," Mema murmured. Grandfather patted her thigh.

"Oh, Ali, I love you deeply. I truly do," Velma said, drawing a hand to her heart. "But sometimes… Do you remember the rest of that experience?"

Rankin snorted.

"Yes, I defended Father…" I glanced around my family. "… from your charges."

I had.

Velma had been the first to regain her senses. "Father's excitement over this woman might be other than what it appears."

I grappled to put words to what I'd just experienced, but I forced out the few I gathered. "What do you mean?"

"Father's been bored since he retired," Velma continued. "But have you noticed that he's been more cheerful lately? Reclaiming lost territory did that for him before. I can't imagine it wouldn't again."

I furrowed my brow as she scanned the room.

"Emperor Altairn has declared war on the nonmagical nations surrounding Elementis. I believe Father plans to leverage Delcina to get insight into the man's thoughts and plans as she weaves the human's dreams. I gave him an advantage when I did it for him with the emperor's ancestor. It would give him an advantage against the other Dream regents this time, too."

"With all due respect, that's quite a leap, sister," Roldan, my brother who looked most like Father, said. "Do you have proof, or are you speculating?"

"I'm speculating."

Such a dire prediction. As the eldest and seemingly most responsible of my siblings, I loved Velma deeply, but she had a way of overthinking things and sucking all the joy out. She meant well, but I hated it when she spoke poorly of Father, bad behavior or no.

Yes, Father had become unpredictable of late, but I chose to still believe the best of him. No, he'd been letting loose, inappropriately so, but in his unique style, and that's what had improved his mood. No matter how repulsive, everyone deserved to let go every now and again without being judged for it. Velma was wrong, she had to be, she did... and I wished she'd stop.

"At least he had a smile on his face. It's been a long time," I threw out. I had to offer an alternative interpretation.

Rankin, a born leader among us, stood and smiled at me. "No offense, Ali, but only you would see a rainbow in what we just experienced."

Several of my siblings had grinned and shaken their heads.

Velma gave a sad smile. "You thought his behavior was acceptable. That he loved Delcina."

I hadn't thought Father's behavior was acceptable, but I wouldn't argue. "To this sun we still don't know who was right." It was true. We didn't know how Father's and Delcina's story would turn out. They were still an item, and the war had ended.

"Give him time. Emperor Altairn is still very much alive and Delcina still weaves his dreams," Velma countered.

Mema held up her hands. "Nothing is going to be accomplished with arguing. But Alissandra, you are right that we don't fall in love with our charges... In that, or in any other fashion for that matter. I suggest you wipe these silly notions from your head and focus on what the prince needs: clear thinking, sound sleep, and a pleasant dream or two."

"Don't worry, it's not like that," I said, forcing a smile. "Really..."

Chapter Thirteen

"Emperor Altairn died," Mema said by way of greeting this breakfast as she took a seat before the place setting at the head of the table, in the private dining room. A steward draped a cloth napkin across her lap then filled her favorite cup with coffee.

I sucked in a breath. Kovis. It had been three annums since the war had ended and life had returned to a less worrisome routine, well, except for his siblings. But the cause of their troubles had just died. I didn't know if I should rejoice or cry.

I looked down the table and locked eyes with Alfreda. Her shoulders slumped, no doubt sad for Kennan, but then she exhaled loudly, as if relieved. She was as conflicted as I.

After what that man had put Kovis and his siblings through... I stifled a growl. But the man was still their father. Yes... their father. And they were now orphans—which was worse, your elders both gone, or both alive but not around much? I sighed and pushed back my roiling emotions.

No matter that I couldn't stand the man, poor Delcina. We all knew the ache of losing a charge.

My eyes dropped to my food. While I'd wanted to, I hadn't gotten close to Delcina with her staying with Father at his palace.

I swallowed hard. Amelia, the nurturing one's, chin trembled. Deor pressed a fist to her lips. The rest of my sisters behaved similarly.

"We'll see her at family fortnight dinner later," Ailith, my ever-inspiring sister, said. "We'll give her hugs and try to encourage her."

Phina and Farfelee nodded their agreement.

Mema frowned, clutching her fork. "No, we won't."

We all looked to Mema with furrowed brows.

"She left."

"Left? What do you mean, left?" I asked.

Mema shook her head. "I shouldn't say, but you'll find out soon enough. Your Father sent her away."

"What? Why?" We all clamored.

I glanced at Velma. She still stared at her plate. At length she said in a low voice, "Because she'll be assigned a new charge and will be of no use to him anymore."

Mema and Velma shared a sorrowful look.

He'd used her. The notion struck a sour chord in my mind, and my mouth dropped open. But I'd been so sure. No one could be that uncaring, or so I'd thought. Poor Delcina. What was Father thinking? He was better than this.

No, Velma, Mema, they had to be wrong. This couldn't be my father. I knew him. But what if they *were* right? I blew out a breath. How could he behave so differently than the male I knew?

The male I thought I knew...

● ● ●

Chapter Fourteen

We celebrated the autumn equinox this sun, and I'd never been less excited. Creepy, crazy Uncle Thao—technically my great uncle and Grandfather's twin—was hosting.

He was one of several members of my extended family who weren't invited to most functions, and justifiably so. Holiday parties he attended were always awkward with his morbid humor, obnoxious laugh, and repeated demands for his favorite beverage, spiced blood. It was best, he claimed, when drunk on a battlefield just after a human conflict—something about the victim's terror or fear gave it the best flavor. Disgusting. He, alone, enjoyed war.

We launched into the chill air and I pulled my jacket tight. I'd nearly fallen out of my chair when Mema said we could wear our flying leathers rather than fancy gowns. None of us maidens had dared ask why, lest she change her mind, but we hadn't objected.

But in no time, we set down outside Uncle Thao's palace. The three-story mansion sprawled a good ways across the shoreline, behind. It kept its promise of creepiness with its cracked masonry and dim lighting. Swirling fog in the glow of the half moon added an extra measure of ghoulish macabre. An owl hooted in the thick trees not far away. My brothers surrounded us maidens. Our guards circled my brothers.

Why couldn't we celebrate tonight when the sun rose? Why'd it have to be first thing this morning? I just wanted to weave Kovis's dreams.

Grandfather knocked then led us through the orange—the color of the *dying* sun, Uncle bragged—front door that a steward held open. I clutched Alfreda's hand.

"Welcome, welcome. So good of you to join me for this auspicious occasion," Uncle Thao greeted, in the high-ceilinged entry hall. Six flaming torches were its only illumination. He'd donned a black robe, but hadn't bothered to comb his stringy, gray hair. I swear I saw something bright red move in it and gasped.

He led us down the torch-lit hall and into a large ballroom. Nothing had changed since my last visit. Weapons with dried blood still on the blade, and a knight's suit of armor, complete with the lance that had pierced it, decorated the front of the room. I'd never wanted to know what had happened to the human. Thankfully, he kept the room poorly illuminated with only a dozen or so lanterns, so I couldn't see into the dim.

"Please, help yourselves. There's plenty of food." He motioned to a table nearby decorated with orange favors, piled high with all manner of orange-colored confections. More orange. His twisted way of screwing with us.

"My cook has been *working herself to death* with all these preparations." He pulled a hand over his mouth in dramatic fashion. "Oh, pardon my slip." He wagged his brows, clearly unapologetic at his inappropriate jest.

I huffed. Inappropriate humor as always. He knew we shepherded short-lived humans. Alfreda swallowed hard. Harding rolled his shoulders. Rankin cringed. I wasn't alone.

Considering it was just he and us, his cook had outdone herself. We could have survived for a sennight.

None of us moved and Uncle Thao frowned.

"Why don't you and I have a drink, Brother? A lightning chaser perhaps?" Grandfather stepped forward and put an arm around his twin's shoulders, then walked him to the long bar that ran half the length of the front wall to the right. It stopped at that gruesome suit of armor.

"Think that guy could play a different song?" I whispered to Alfreda, still clutching her hand. The overweight musician puffed a slow dirge on a lysard to the left. It sent chills up my back.

She tilted her head. "Maybe you could get him to accompany you." She nodded at a lute resting near the male.

I nodded and we, along with one of our guards moved near. I cleared my throat and said, "Excuse me, but would you mind if I played that?"

The balding musician smiled—he was missing a front tooth—and said, "Not at all. Here have a seat." He scooted over leaving room for me to sit on the stool beside him.

I pulled the stool farther away and sat. "How about 'Sweet Sleep, Hold me Tight.'" It was a lullaby familiar to most, and while it wouldn't be suitable for dancing, it would put a stop to the dirge he had been playing.

"What's your name?" I asked.

"Easton. You?"

"Call me Ali."

"All right. After you, Ali," he invited, smiling.

I strummed the lute, letting the music lighten my angst. And true to form, as the notes and chords and melody filled the room, my soul calmed.

Easton accompanied and together we strummed life into our gloomy surroundings. My siblings soon joined us, singing along to the host of familiar lullabies. By the time we'd played ten tunes, everyone had relaxed. Not enough to eat or drink any of Uncle Thao's food, but we were no longer jumping at every strange sight or sound.

At some point, servants brought chairs for everyone.

"I haven't had this much fun in ages," Easton commented. "All he wants is slow and mournful. It's *killing* me." He grimaced, then looked up. "Please tell me you all don't weave dreams."

We grinned.

He opened his mouth to apologize, but Harding held up a hand. "No offence taken."

"Play another," Farfelee begged. Mema smiled.

And so we did.

Father clapped several songs later from behind us. We'd been having so much fun that none of us had heard him arrive. "That's the cheeriest music I've *ever* heard in this place."

Grandfather and Uncle joined us.

"You're ruining the mood," Uncle Thao complained.

"On the contrary, it's the best I've ever heard here." Father nodded to emphasize his point.

"You can't jus... come in here and t... take over my music." Uncle slurred his words. Clearly, Grandfather had helped him loosen up. Probably so we could leave early.

Grandfather winked at Mema. She'd noticed, too.

"We didn't take it over, Uncle," I defended. "Everyone's having a good time."

"It seems everyone prefers this over the other music," Grandfather encouraged.

"You took it over." Thao wasn't going to let this go, and I looked to Father.

Uncle belched, then forced a laugh. "How would you like me taking over Wake some night? Yeah, that's what I shou... do."

"Uncle, you don't know what you're saying. Wake is not remotely the same as the music in your gruesome ballroom." Father frowned, but then his expression turned thoughtful.

I furrowed my brow, not understanding the change in him. What was he considering?

"You don... like my decorating? How dare you."

Things were devolving quickly.

"Perhaps we should go," Grandfather suggested.

• • •

"Perhaps you shoul... Good riddance to the lot of you." Uncle Thao swatted the air.

Father motioned a servant over to attend to his master, and once Thao had swagger-stumbled out of hearing, he said, "Shall we?"

He didn't have to ask twice.

I turned to Easton. "Thank you. You made this at least a small celebration. You should come work for Father."

"I would like that very much."

I looked and Father nodded.

"Ask for me at the palace of sandmaidens," I said.

"I'll do that, thank you so much."

Heartbeats later, we flew over the flickering lights of Sand City. Chatter filled the air although I noticed Father was quiet, as he had been since Thao made that comment. Was he still thinking of Uncle? Why would that dreadful relation bring up conquering Wake? A shiver ran down my back. And it wasn't from the wind.

Yes, there was probably much for him to consider. Family politics had definitely taken a turn for the worse.

The only question... how much worse?

Chapter Fifteen

The sun was halfway down to the horizon when I summoned my courage and reached for the hulking iron doorknocker. The thing was a grotesque gargoyle head with one empty eye socket. The other socket housed one bloodshot, bulging eye. A forked tongue extended, frozen in time. I grabbed the ring that it held in its mouth, raised it, then released it quickly. Its thud reverberated against the wood sending a chill down my back, squelching my giddiness at spending time with Father, as it always did.

Father's palace was situated on the northwestern coast of the island and the sound of the waves thundering against the sandy shore only served to reinforce my angst. I glanced about, my hands growing sweaty. He housed 'domesticated' mares here.

It was a sore subject. Father had shepherded human dreams for eons and knew the ferocity of these creatures to inflict untold terror on our charges. How he even considered such a thing... If I didn't know him like I did, I might feel betrayed, as if he'd sided with the enemy.

Inducers of nightmares, mares preyed on human fears, changing from this, their usual form, into whatever most terrified our charges. For better or worse, humans couldn't sense their presence, only experience the terror they brought. Once a mare had a charge in its control, I was powerless to help until he or she woke. Mares were menaces, pure and simple.

A loud bang, then shouts, to the right drew my attention to the ancient outbuilding where he housed them. My knees grew shaky. My guards shifted behind me, equally on edge.

Open the damn door.

Metal clanked against metal.

Snarling.

And a very large, wolf-like beast raced from behind the place, trainers yelling, running after, on its fluffy tail.

I yelped. My protectors whirled around, drew their swords, and took ready positions.

The mare's purple fur glowed even in the waning sun as it bounded toward me. It might have been pretty if it wasn't so terrifying.

The beast bared its long, white teeth and snapped its jaws as it sped closer.

I ducked down, behind my guards, heart racing.

The creature slowed to a trot as it neared the porch. I gulped down breaths to stay quiet.

It stopped, then dropped to its front quarters in a crouch, mammoth paws outstretched as the trainers caught up, panting.

A putrid stench, like eggs rotting, hit me and I thought I might retch.

"It's not time to play Warin," one of the trainers said, as he and his fellow handler surrounded the purple monster.

What?

I peeked out from behind my guard. The mare leapt up, placing its forepaws on either side of the trainer's neck.

"Whoa, boy. Down."

The other trainer approached and had nearly slipped a rope around the beast's head when it morphed, becoming a...

I shrieked. It had taken on the image of the grotesque gargoyle doorknocker behind me—one eye socket was empty, the other had a bloodshot, bulging eye. A forked tongue flicked in and out.

"That's enough Warin." The trainer pulled the rope tight and turned on his heels, the creature in tow.

The other trainer waved. "Sorry to frighten you."

I, and my guards, exhaled.

Only then did a black liveried servant open the creepy door. He extended an open palm inviting us in.

"Please wait here while I announce your arrival."

My pulse slowed and my breathing eased as I waited. Damn monster. Why had Father decided to domesticate those menaces? I mean, I knew why—he'd gotten bored with retirement and taken up the challenge of taming a few, for security purposes, or so he'd said—but still.

Father finally appeared and strode to a stop, dressed in a casual black tunic and coordinating breeches with gold accents that did nothing to hide his ever-increasing girth since retiring.

"Alissandra, pardon my delay. I hope you weren't waiting long." He smiled but didn't elaborate on what had kept him, just reciprocated my hug. I wouldn't mention the scare his damn mare had caused, it being a sore subject, mentioning it would only put him in a bad mood.

"You're here early."

I grinned. "I couldn't sleep, so we left early."

He smiled. "Well, I'm excited to spend time with you, too. In fact, I thought we might try something new this sun."

I cocked my head and he wagged his eyebrows. He was in a good mood for a change. I wouldn't question what had brought it on; I'd just enjoy it.

"Follow me." His request came over his shoulder.

I motioned for my guards to remain.

We passed his throne room, a huge and ostentatious affair. I didn't care for his decorating style—gaudy, gold, and garish. It lacked the sophistication and richness of the diverse cultures of the regions

I'd visited in Father's territory and seemed a blunt force effort to prove his power to anyone who approached him seated there.

I much preferred the simple. Nice, perhaps elegant with the right occasion, but simple.

I followed him past the dining room where he'd shown off Delcina so long ago. I still couldn't believe he'd told her to leave like he had. Why? Why had he really sent her away? Velma had speculated, but I couldn't settle with her explanation.

We entered his drawing room, a multi-windowed room looking out at the sea. Three onyx-colored sofas with a short table in their midst occupied the farthest reaches of the room to the left. A hulking ebony desk stood closer. Books lined the entirety of the wall to the right. Had it not been for the sun streaming through the huge windows, this room would have been dark and menacing with its java-colored wood floors, heavy wood trim, and midnight blue rugs. It was every bit as masculine as he.

"I've been thinking about ways to help our humans. I'd like you to help me try something," he said.

That sounded promising. "What do you need me to do?"

"Help me peek into your human's mind and see what he loves most dearly."

I hesitated. After the way he'd treated Delcina, I wasn't sure. "I can *tell* you that."

"No, I need to access his mind myself. I know you can grant me that because you're very capable."

He'd said he wanted to help humans. But why would he need direct access? How would it help?

Still I dithered.

"What more noble a cause could there be? I wouldn't ask for your help if I didn't need it, Alissandra." I flinched when he reached out and cradled my face in a hand.

He was asking for *my* help. I drew a hand over my heart. "Okay, I'll help you. What do you need me to do?"

"Hand me his thought thread."

I gave him a long look, but finally nodded.

* * *

I reached out with my mind and pictured the dream canopy. Then I went to Kovis and grabbed the thread of his thoughts. I smiled. Despite it being daytime, my prince permitted me entrance. I'd never attempted to allow anyone else access to his thread and wasn't sure how to accomplish it. I tried one thing, then another with neither working.

I knew what the issue was. Kovis and I shared a link—every sand person was linked to their dream charge at the time of assignment and that link didn't sever until their charge passed on—but it made it nearly impossible to accomplish what Father sought to do. I tried a couple more things, and again failed.

"This isn't easy, Father," I said, wiping my brow.

"I appreciate your effort. Just keep trying."

My head started to ache after several more tries, but I persevered and inspiration finally struck. Father reached out and held Kovis's thread for himself. But it took concentration to keep it open while Father took a peek.

"His sister and brother are who he holds most dear," Father said some time later.

I exhaled, releasing the thread. "Yes, he's been deeply hurt by his father." I wouldn't mention a certain woman who had recently crushed his heart. I huffed to myself all the same. "His siblings are what give him the strength to go on."

I was exhausted after all that mental work and yawned.

"Shall we take a break? How about we take a walk down by the shore?"

My eyes went wide and Father chuckled. "Don't worry, we won't run into any mares."

I exhaled and slowly nodded.

I ended up staying the night so we could continue our work.

The next sun, when we reconvened in his drawing room, Father asked, "So my beautiful daughter, you proved yourself very capable, are you up for another challenge?"

I hesitated, but not long enough for Father to notice. "Sure, if it'll help our humans."

Father looked into my eyes with love. "You're so smart."

I savored his praise. Although in the back of my mind, I wondered how this was going to help our humans.

"I need to see what it would take for your human to betray what he most loves."

I clenched my jaw. "I don't want to hurt him." Why would this be beneficial? What purpose would it serve?

"Oh it won't. I just need access to his memories."

I furrowed my brow.

"I know you care about your human."

"Shouldn't I?"

"Absolutely, but I promise not to cause him pain, my sweet girl." Father winked.

I sighed. "All right, then." I was faster this time and let Father hold Kovis's thought thread within a few heartbeats.

I panted by the time Father left, but he praised, "Well done, my brilliant daughter. And see, no harm to him. You have such a good heart. That's why you've become my favorite."

"Your favorite?" I beamed and forgot my tiredness.

"You are, Alissandra, and I don't say that lightly." He held up a finger. "I will only call you that in private though. We don't want to make your siblings jealous."

Whether he called me his favorite publicly or only in private, I didn't care. I had become special to him, among all my siblings. I grinned.

I couldn't wait to see what our work yielded. Would it truly help humans? How I hoped it would.

———————

"Would you like to know what all our hard work is leading us to?" Father asked. I'd returned to his palace on and off over the last two moons and we'd made good progress.

Tonight, we'd finally gotten Kovis to raise his arm while sleeping. I was resting after expending nearly everything I had. But we'd done it. Just the two of us.

"As you know, wild mares have plagued humans. I want to free them from the nightmares these beasts cause."

But Father bred and sheltered mares. He fostered their very existence. The thought flitted through my mind, but my excitement made it evaporate before I could examine it.

"The problem is no one human's mind is strong enough to drive off a wild mare. I need to bind their minds together so that, collectively, they will be able to overcome this menace. That's why we've been working on allowing me to access your charge's thought thread while you control his movements. If I can gather several threads together at the same time, the humans should be strong enough to thwart mares."

"That's brilliant, Father." To rid dream charges of those insidious beasts. Forever. We'd always been powerless to them, but Father sought a way to free humans. He didn't have to ask twice; I'd do *whatever* it took.

My gut balked, refusing to buy what I was selling. I ignored it.

We'd free humans, me and Father. We would.

Chapter Sixteen

My stomach twisted as I scanned the crowds from the balcony of Father's palace. Raucous hoots. Profane shouts. They were getting vulgar. And mares lurked. I couldn't see them, but I knew they were here, somewhere.

It seemed nearly everyone in Father's realm was here. And libations were flowing.

I covered a yawn. Like the crowds, I'd tried to stay up all sun, but it was quickly catching up with me.

I ran a hand over my shimmery new dress, the one made for the winter solstice ball commemorating the shortest sun of the solar cycle that we celebrated. And a queen would be named.

Wasila elbowed me. "Rainbows and sunshine, your dress will bare wear marks if you don't stop running your hands over it."

"But it's so pretty. It practically glows in the sun."

She chuckled. "I know, and the colors are bright like Mother wears." I hadn't said it that much, had I?

"But they are."

"I love your enthusiasm."

I returned a smile as she took a sip of her Sparkling Passion and leaned back against the balcony rail.

"Come on, let's go vote." I grabbed her hand and dragged her through Father's palace, past his creepy front door knocker and outside into the warm air—times like this made me appreciate Dream's always-balmy temperatures. They were so different than what my charges endured in Wake for several moons an annum, or so I'd deduced.

We stopped at the ballot box situated on a small linen-covered table to the left of a temporary stage that had been erected on the front lawn of the palace for the occasion. "May we please have ballots?"

The liveried servant bobbed his head and handed us parchment and quills.

"You know who you're going to nominate for queen?" Wasila asked, wagging her brows.

I snickered. I'd only been going on and on about Beval's gown. My sister had outdone herself with her artistry this time, actually creating the fabric her dress was made from. It seemed to change color as she moved. She wouldn't tell anyone how she'd done it, and I was envious.

Wasila hid her parchment while she wrote her candidate, then folded it and dropped it in the slot in the top of the ballot box. I stuck out my tongue, snickering, as I dropped mine in.

"Sisters!" Ailith waved a hand not far away.

Wasila and I joined her, along with Wynnfrith and Deor.

"Thought we'd wait here for Father to announce the winner," Ailith said. "Front row view and all."

I snagged a wild-boar-wrapped sea serpent finger bite from a passing servant and popped it in my mouth.

"Have you seen Mother?" I asked, covering my mouth with a hand.

My four siblings all shook their heads.

"She never comes," Wynnfrith said.

"Can't imagine she would, not with Father crowning a Solstice queen," Ailith added. "Drives her crazy. I mean come on, the 'queen,' whoever it is, isn't even old enough to have offspring. I think she feels insulted."

I frowned. "There've been older 'queens' named."

"Not over a thousand-annums old," Wasila said. "Think back."

I did, to find she was right. Huh. "Well, it's not like Father's going to marry the Solstice Ball queen and replace her."

"All the same. I think she takes it personally," Wasila said, taking another sip of the drink she still nursed.

"I think she secretly wishes Father would just up and marry her," Deor added. My siblings nodded.

I'd just popped another finger bite in my mouth when the noise of the crowd intensified, then broke into wild clapping. A few whistles accented the applause.

Father strode on stage with a folded parchment in hand. He stopped in the center and ruffled his immaculately groomed, onyx wings. "Who will become my next queen?" He wagged his brows.

Laughter erupted and thoughts of his dinner with Delcina bolted to mind.

He held up his hands and cleared his throat. "But in all seriousness, I have the determination of our illustrious judges."

I grabbed Ailith's arm. She looked over at me, smiling.

Please say Beval. Please say Beval.

A hush fell over those gathered.

"Are you ready for me to crown our Winter Solstice Queen?" Father scanned the anxious crowd, then laughed. "You're all so serious."

A round of chuckles rose.

"Third place goes to Ebba." Cheers went up. "Please come and receive your prize, this beautiful bouquet." He nodded at the abundant flowers a steward standing beside him held.

A beautiful maiden dressed in a bright red, A-line gown wove her way through the crowd. Tall and slender, it was no wonder she'd

· · ·

had so many nominate her. She was striking, to be sure. She beamed, but remained poised as she climbed the steps and accepted the gift.

"Second place goes to…" Father looked around. "Raisa. I hope I'm pronouncing that correctly. Come, receive your prize."

Cheers followed the maiden who was clad in a shiny silver gown. She smiled broadly and accepted another, bigger bouquet, grinning.

Father cleared his throat. "And the winner and queen of this winter solstice ball is…" He smiled as his eyes read the name, but remained silent for several heartbeats longer, no doubt to create maximum drama. "My very own daughter, Alissandra. Come."

I threw a hand over my mouth. Ailith, Wynnfrith, Wasila and Deor clapped wildly beside me. I'd won. I couldn't believe it. My family and maybe a few others had thought that much of me. I couldn't wrap my head around it. They loved me so much.

Deor nudged me, returning me to my beaming senses. I took a deep breath. I could do this. I climbed the steps up to the stage and made my way to Father who beamed right along with me.

At length, he motioned for quiet, then removed a thin gold tiara from the cushion that a waiting steward held on a pillow in his gloved hands. Father turned and stepped forward. As he placed it on my head he whispered, "Congratulations, my favorite daughter."

He drew a hand behind his back, and then with his other, he took mine and kissed the back. "Queen of the ball, will you honor me with the first dance?"

Such a rare treat, and he was an amazing dancer. I bobbed my head.

We descended the steps and my siblings circled around, cheering and clapping. Stewards relieved Father and me of our crowns, and I entrusted my shoes to their keeping as well.

"Which dance would you like to do?" Father asked.

It took no thought. I loved to watch him do The Altairn, a dance he had invented as a nod to the altairn, a large bird of prey that inhabited Wake realm. The dance mimicked their mating ritual, locking talons and spinning in flight. Father always made it look so smooth and sophisticated.

He winked. "Very well. Are you ready?"

I nodded and a smile eclipsed my face.

We launched into the skies taking care to avoid each other's wings. The crowd's cheers faded as we soared up through the clouds. I squinted, everything was so bright with the sun out.

Despite the rushing wind, I heard him say, "You look beautiful, Alissandra."

My smile widened. "Thank you, Father. You look rather dashing yourself."

Looking down he said, "This old thing?"

"You do," I insisted. He'd had a new tunic and jacket tailored to his heftier frame and it made him look thinner, or at least not his usual, of late, frumpy self.

He laughed.

We continued beating our wings, higher and higher and higher. Father always pushed the limits. It was one of the things I loved about him. Unlike Mema, he never put down my ideas, but encouraged my creativity.

I danced plenty, but this was higher than I'd ever danced before. I chanced a look down. Father's castle looked like a toy that Kovis might have played with when little. The crowd of sand people spilling from every available space looked like gnats. I could see all the way over to the palace of sandmaidens, and Mema and Grandfather's place next to the palace of sandmen.

"We're nearly to the dream canopy," Father yelled over the wind. The sun caressed the transparent, scrim-like canopy I reached my mind out to every time I wove dreams—its presence shielded Dream from Wake's detection.

Excitement welled up in me. It's what I reached my thoughts out to every night. But as we soared into the cloudy layer, dizziness assaulted my head. I couldn't tell which way was up or down. I grabbed Father hoping he'd steady me. While he drew me close, vertigo didn't relent and I felt bile rise in my throat.

● ● ●

"Don't you love it?" he asked, looking about, soaking in the sights. "I only do this once an annum. I like to make it as thrilling as I can, for both of us."

I swallowed hard and shook my head. A chill slithered up my back. "I don't feel well. Can we get out of…" I must have been green because Father took one look at my face and we descended to just below the canopy where we hovered.

The heartbeat we dropped out of the hazy space, my head cleared and I took a deep breath.

"Better? Just the inversion between Dream and Wake. It can disorient."

"Yes," I said on the exhale, still regaining my bearings.

"You've got a sensitive stomach, that's too bad. I love to soar higher, but no matter. Do you think you're ready to dance?"

"Give me a few heartbeats."

He smiled one of his winning smiles and my stomach calmed. "Okay, I'm ready," I told him not long after.

He dug into the breast pocket of his jacket and pulled out an ankle band—it looked like an overgrown hair band. "Allow me to put it on you first."

I fluttered, cinched the ribbon in the hem of my gown so my skirt wouldn't fly up as we descended, and extended my bare feet.

A few heartbeats later, he'd bound his ankles, too, and we jerked each other as we attempted hovering.

"Get into sync. On my count, bring your wings down."

I did and our strokes evened as we hovered.

"Would you like to select our music?" he asked.

I drew a hand to my chest. "Definitely. I feel close to the gods"— he raised a brow—"I think harp."

"Very well." He let the corners of his mouth rise, then locked onto my mind in a manner similar to how I connected with each charge's thought thread. I felt his presence stroke me as he imagined a harpist. Then wonderful, ethereal chords began filling our connection.

"Ready?"

I bit my lip. "As I'll ever be."

He chuckled, then dove headfirst. Tied together, his motion catapulted us into a roll, and I shrieked.

But after the initial plunge to gain momentum, Father slowed us to a lazy pace so I could take in the sun, the clouds, birds that flew by, the lushness of our island—so small compared to the vastness of Father's Dream realm, yet so beautiful. Rock outcroppings sprouted in the surrounding sea that was as clear and blue as Kovis's eyes. I could see the bottom where it was shallower.

We continued our gentle dance and I looked back up to where we'd been, where I'd gotten dizzy. Only this high up could I see the canopy's shimmer and then only when at the right angle—my gown could have been its twin.

I savored every heartbeat of this experience, but the ground grew closer and I motioned to untie us.

Father shook his head and beamed. "My favorite part."

My heart started beating faster.

Closer. I kicked my feet, trying to free them.

Father again shook his head. "Trust me."

Nearer. I swallowed hard.

Father remained calm. "Do you trust me?"

I tried bending to reach my ankles, but our increased momentum forbade it.

"I'll take care of us as soon as you trust me. Show me. Relax."

My breathing sped and I fought the tether. Still the ground raced to meet us.

He locked eyes with me. "Trust me, Alissandra."

A command. I squeezed my eyes shut and, against my best judgment, went slack.

I felt my legs free a heartbeat later, and I screamed, free-falling.

Chapter Seventeen

"Your charge *will* betray those he most loves," Father said for the fifth time, growing louder against my protests. "And you will help me discover how."

"What does that have to do with driving off mares?" I shot back.

I'd stayed after the ball and spent the next sun resting from that harrowing experience. My heart still raced at the memory.

I'd screamed as I hurtled toward the ground, faster and faster. Closer and closer. Straining. Resisting Hades with every fiber of my being.

In the end, in that very last heartbeat, Father's strong arms had surrounded me and drawn me against his abundant chest. I'd hugged him plenty, but his arms had never felt so solid, so steady, so stable. He'd caught me. No, he'd captured me. Ripped me from Hades' maw.

And as his feet hit the ground and he carried me to a jogging stop, he'd whispered, "Well done, Alissandra. I'm proud of you."

We'd been so close to the ground. So very close. If I'd hesitated a heartbeat longer... My stomach tensed even now.

Father took a deep breath and let it out. "Driving off mares is the end goal, but as I mentioned, no one human's mind is strong enough to accomplish it on their own. By determining what it would take for your charge to betray those he loves, it will allow me to assess how strong his mind is. If it doesn't take much, I'll know his mind is weak. If it takes a lot, I'll know he's strong. Mares are tenacious. If we are to succeed, the combined threads must be robust."

"But I don't want to hurt Kovis."

"Have you or I ever hurt him?"

"Well, no."

"I know you love your charge. I promise this won't hurt him." He winked.

I gave him a long look. He'd been honest, explaining why he felt it was necessary to test the strength of Kovis's mind. I had to admit, against the ravages of mares, it made sense.

I nodded, and handed him my Dreambeam's thought thread.

Father worked for some time, but when he finally left Kovis's mind, he praised me, "Well done, my brilliant daughter. And see, no harm to him. You have such a good heart."

"What did you find?"

"Nothing yet, but I'll keep working on it."

I smiled. I wasn't surprised Father hadn't determined the lengths that would be necessary for Kovis to betray someone he loved. Kovis held those he loved close and once he committed himself, he never betrayed them. At least not that I'd seen.

I huffed. I wished the same could be said for everyone Kovis loved: His father. His lover. Not Amice. Never Amice. She'd been only sweet—it hadn't been her fault that Kovis had been young and inexperienced and the relationship hadn't gone anywhere. No, another lover, the duplicitous wench. I refused even to think on her name. I growled. They'd both crushed his heart, in different ways, but the result had been the same. And now I had my hands full trying to thaw his frozen heart.

I just hoped I could.

"We've accomplished much. Are you ready for something different, Alissandra?" Father said settling on the sofa beside me in his drawing room a sennight later.

"Sure." He'd still not determined what it would take for Kovis to betray someone he loved. I smiled to myself. And he never would.

"I want you to make your charge scratch his face, like he has an itch."

I chuckled. "Really? Why?"

"You got him to raise his arm, but I need you to perfect your ability to control his movements. It's very important."

I furrowed my brow as he picked up a report to read while I worked. He hadn't answered my question. Why would it be important to better control his movements? How would that help humans overcome mares? I'd no idea, but his scowl as he read that report told me he wasn't in a mood to ask. So I set to work.

After two unsuccessful tries, I interrupted him, "What if I can't do it?"

He peered over the top of the parchment. "You're brilliant, my favorite daughter. I know you can succeed if you put your mind to it."

After two more attempts, I asked, "I've only ever controlled *my* dream charge's thread, how are you going to hold several together at once?"

He smiled. "Don't you worry about that. I'm working on it."

I raised a brow. He was working on it? How? With another sand being? His grumble, at what he read, made me hold my questions.

I got Kovis to touch his nose, but nearly made his nail scratch him as he'd moved his hand away."

"What if I make him draw blood? I don't want to hurt him, Father."

He frowned. "Then you'll need to be more careful." His voice held warning.

After another attempt, I asked, "How can you be sure connecting thought threads won't alter a charge's thoughts? Could humans transfer thoughts and think they are their own? That could be disastrous."

Father took a deep breath and let it out slowly. "All these questions, Alissandra. I need you to trust me."

I fidgeted as he eyed me up and down.

At length he asked, "Do you remember our dance during solstice?"

In a heartbeat, that panicked, out-of-control feeling of our dance that had seared into my memory, bolted to the front of my mind. My breathing labored. I gripped the arm of the sofa.

"Calm, Alissandra."

And just like that, the security and safety of feeling Father's strong arms surrounding and protecting me in the end, overwhelmed. No matter that he'd caused it, he'd been my savior.

I took a deep breath and let it out slowly.

Father would never hurt me. He'd only, ever save me.

He smiled then reached over and patted my thigh as I looked into his russet eyes.

He'd never hurt anyone I loved either. Ridding humans of mares. It would be good for them. What more noble a cause could there be?

I'd successfully gotten Kovis to scratch his cheek—without drawing blood—rub his eye, and tap his lips while sleeping.

Father and I had celebrated, just the two of us. We'd both been ecstatic.

I sighed, again savoring our accomplishments as I sat on the sofa in Father's drawing room, waiting for him to join me so we could start work. How I loved spending time with him. What's more, he seemed to be enjoying our time, too. I hadn't seen him laugh so much in ages and it made me happy.

Would he have me make Kovis rub his stomach while he slept this night? I smiled, considering the possibility.

Father's face held no amusement as he sat down beside me a while later.

I furrowed my brow.

"We need to see if we can get your charge to cut himself with a knife while he sleeps."

I sat back. "What? Why?" My stomach twisted at the thought.

"Defeating mares will be a terrifying thing, and we need to ensure he's up to it. This is just another part of testing how strong his mind is. Having him cut himself should test his ability to endure harm to himself, willingly."

"But you promised you'd never hurt him."

He held up a hand. "You know I wouldn't if we didn't have to, but I've thought hard and can't deduce another way, especially since I wasn't able to accomplish it by delving into his mind to determine what would make him betray a loved one. The cut won't be deep."

"It's because Kovis will never betray someone he loves." I nodded sharply.

Father's half smile vanished as quickly as it came.

Supposed need aside, this was wrong. He'd promised not to hurt Kovis, and he'd just crossed that line—there was *no way* I would *ever* allow him or anyone else to harm my Dreambeam. No way.

"Now let's proceed." It wasn't a question.

I wanted to shake my head, but resisted the urge.

I needed to stay calm, pretend I wasn't alarmed. Father would only become more insistent if I did.

I cleared my throat. "That's a lot more complicated. Raising an arm and doing all those other things is one thing, but cutting himself... it's entirely different. He'll not only have to sit up, but also have to grab his blade, and then actually cut himself. I don't know if I can manage it."

"I need you to try, Alissandra. You are my favorite daughter and enjoy all the benefits that holds." He raised a brow.

My stomach twisted. What was he saying?

I needed to stall. I'd eventually get him around to my view. I would. But until then...

My heart raced as I nodded. "Okay, Father, I'll try." And I pretended to, even adding grunts to show how much energy I exerted.

———————

"You're not trying hard enough," Father said, frowning, several suns later. "You easily made your human move his extremities, what could possibly be so difficult?"

I huffed. He'd promised not to hurt Kovis, and he'd broken that promise.

"As I've told you, getting Kovis to cut himself is a lot more complicated. I have to get him to sit up. Then while holding him there, I have to make him grab his blade, and while maintaining all that, he has to unsheathe the blade, look at his arm, then bring it down and actually cut himself. I've never attempted a series of movements, let alone one in which he willingly harms himself."

Father blew out a long breath.

I didn't care that I frustrated him. He'd eventually tire and see reason. I would wait him out.

It had worked before.

Chapter Eighteen

I let out a breath. What would this sunset bring? Father and I still didn't see eye to eye and, as a result, it had been a sennight since I'd last seen him, but he was joining us for breakfast.

I pushed worry aside as I entered the dining room, joining Mema and my sisters. It seemed I was the last of my siblings to arrive, and I'd barely finished giving Mema a kiss when Father strode through the doors. I pivoted to give him a hug.

"Mema and I need to talk about important matters," he said as he brushed past. He greeted Mema, giving her a peck on either cheek.

I forced a smile, then took a seat between Wasila and Farfelee.

Some time later, I put my napkin down and listened to Father and Mema discuss plans for the upcoming Festival of Sandlings. Their conversation seemed to go on and on.

"You may be dismissed, Alissandra," Mema said as I started tapping my finger on the table.

"Oh. No. Sorry. Father, I need to speak with you once you're done."

Mema frowned. "Then you'll have to be still."

Everyone else had left. Velma and Wynnfrith had given me questioning looks as they headed out the dining room doors.

At length, they concluded and Mema left. Father turned to me. "What is it that can't wait?" His tone was sharp.

I took a deep breath to compose my thoughts then looked Father in the eye.

He let out a huff.

I asked, "Have a done something to offend you Father? Things seem different between us, and I am unsure why."

I figured he'd deny it, but instead he said, "Show me you love me more than your charge."

"What?" I was stunned silent, his accusation that I could love another more than him was absurd.

He was putting himself in direct opposition to my charge. He'd *never* done that before. Ever.

"You're hedging and not trying your hardest when we work together. I can see it in your eyes," he continued.

I drew in a breath. I needed to stand up for Kovis. Father needed to know I didn't support him in this, no matter how noble the cause.

"Yes, Father, you're right. I am hedging. I don't feel good about hurting my charge. You promised me that Kovis wouldn't be harmed, and you broke it."

He shook his head. "You let me know when you're ready to put me first and we'll resume our work to rid humans of mares." He brushed past me without another word.

My heart climbed into my throat. I loved Father, but I would never betray my charge. He was innocent and I could never willingly hurt him.

Chapter Nineteen

Breakfast with Father hadn't gone well, not long ago. His brush off still smarted, but I refused to cave. So how would fortnight family dinner go this morn? I tried to push the thought away as I scanned the large, high-ceilinged dining room. My sisters and I hosted dinner this sunrise.

Nearly every one of my siblings seemed in good spirits as we waited for all of us to assemble. We mingled in the open area to the left of the one long table that ran the length of the room. Even Mema let a corner of her mouth hitch up at Rankin's joke—it was so unlike her. It seemed we were all ready to blow off some steam and relax after the nights we'd had weaving our charges' dreams.

I waved at Easton, the musician we'd freed from crazy Uncle Thao's employ not long ago. He reciprocated, smiling. He and another male played in the front corner of the room, Easton a lute, the other male, a rebec. They seemed to have picked up on our moods because they favored us with upbeat selections. A steward stopped near them and relit one of the army of candles that illuminated the otherwise dim room.

I adjusted a sleeve on my dress and took a sip of my thunder sour—yes, I was really letting loose. Good, because I needed to. The drink wasn't bad. A little too sour though and I ruffled my wings.

Harding stopped next to me. He'd dressed like most of my brothers in a tailored, dark, casual shirt and pants and had rolled up the sleeves to his elbows. A feather wafted up as he ruffled his black wings, then threw an arm around my shoulder and pecked my cheek. I loved Harding. He was laid-back unless something threatened someone or something he valued, like us.

"How's it going, little sister?" He winked. I playfully swatted his arm as my cheeks warmed—little traitors.

"Fine. And Kovis is doing well also," I said, grinning.

He snorted.

I hadn't seen him, well most of my brothers actually, since last dinner, not surprising since we were all busy with our own work, not to mention living in different places.

I scanned my family and held back a sigh as I noticed Mother was absent again. She rarely showed up to any of our dinners.

We just waited for Father and a couple others. My stomach tensed. I hadn't told anyone about the tension that had been building between us over the last moon and a half, and I felt alone. I was probably naïve, but I still hoped the situation would resolve itself. Judging by his recent actions, it seemed he wasn't about to let our disagreement go either.

My thoughts drifted to Kovis. I'd seen his reflection again earlier as I wove his dreams, it brought a small smile. His royal blue eyes with hazel centers lingered in my consciousness. Bless the Ancient One. I wished I was able to see them more. I chuckled to myself, remembering back to when he'd regularly flexed his muscles and admired his growing chest with those eyes. Oh, mother.

A corner of my mouth hitched up. Whew, I needed to stop fantasizing.

I moved next to Farfelee and clinked glasses with her, schooling my face to keep my daydreaming secret. Ever fun loving, she lived for the moment, and true to form, as Clovis, my baby brother, joined us, a twinkle crept into her eyes. "Nice hair." She exaggerated looking him over, this way and that, examining the two tufts of thick, black hair that stuck straight out from the back of his head.

He'd sculpted it to match his wings, this time. I shook my head. What would he come up with next?

Clovis winked, then drew an arm across his waist and bowed. "I'll take that as a compliment."

"Oh, absolutely." Farfelee covered her mouth but couldn't silence her giggle.

Velma walked through the open doors, spotted me, and headed over. A steward shoved a bubbly drink into her hand as she reached us and gave me a one-arm hug. "How are you?"

While she'd kept the question light, I sensed a deeper, unspoken probing behind her words. Did she know? Had she somehow figured out?

I forced a smile. "Fine. I'm fine." I had to convince myself, or she'd see right through the lie.

Her only reply was a frown. I knew I needed to divert any questions before she dug deeper, so I tuned in to what Keaton was saying. "...yeah, I had fun weaving one dream tonight. My charge, Forestyne—she's sixteen if you remember—went to a celebration. It seems the Altairn princes turned twenty-five. She's sweet on Prince Kovis. She thinks he's, how shall we say, rather handsome with his brooding, good looks. She particularly likes how he fills out a shirt with those bulging muscles."

Wasila snickered and looked my way. She made up for her lack of stature with a playful side, so her not-at-all innocent glance— batting those long, black lashes—drew more looks. "Sounds like you've got competition, Ali." Her comment loosed a round of chuckles from the others.

I felt my cheeks warm again, but replied, "Nothing I can't handle." I forced a smile.

"Ooo." A chorus rose.

Father appeared in the doorway with a scowl etching his face. His sudden stop made the bottom of his black robe swish and drew everyone's attention. All levity died. A muscle on his thick neck bulged as he strode to his place at the head of the table.

Only the sounds of chair legs scrapping against the marble floor filled the space as we moved to our places at the long table. Dawn had not yet broken and the night's blackness amplified Father's mood as it filtered through the floor-to-ceiling window behind his place. Only the crystal chandelier watching over us seemed oblivious to our family dynamics, supporting the candles casting light about.

Father scanned the room but stopped when he reached me. I swallowed hard. No good could come from this. He locked eyes with mine for too long. I wanted to shrink back, to cower, even make myself invisible, not that it would happen, but one could wish.

After what felt like an eternity, he finally thrust his chair back and took his seat. Eadu, normally analytical and less sensitive, gave me a discrete, but reassuring nod from the other side of the table. She didn't know my secret, but if even she was empathizing with me, I was in deeper trouble than I knew.

The server had just set the first course, dragon scale soup, before me when Father launched into his snips—"It seems some of you have been *pretending* that you care about the humans you steward." While he spoke to the room as a whole, he made it abundantly clear who he aimed his comment at. Everyone was forced to sit and listen.

Ailith and Bega sent a sympathetic look. Wasila shifted in her chair. She wasn't alone.

Father, if nothing else, was consistent. Whenever he did something like this, he'd start with indirect comments, and as he worked himself up, he'd move to a direct attack. I'd never been the target, but I'd sat through enough of these to know. I braced for more.

He didn't disappoint. "You think you are so special, don't you?" he said, staring daggers at me as servers brought dreamberry brie bites, the second course.

I inhaled sharply. This dressing down was approaching the peak of what I'd ever heard him dish out. How much further would he take it?

"I thought you were brilliant, but you're not. Your actions tell me your mind needs... enlightenment, Alissandra. It seems not even a candle flickers in that head of yours."

I closed my eyes and focused on breathing as the third course— seahorse cocktail—arrived. The tangy cream sauce I always loved tasted bland, but I forced myself to eat, seeking to hide how he was affecting me.

I didn't know how it was possible, but Father's words grew even more piercing. "Dyeus damn you, Alissandra, putting him before me."

I couldn't shut him out because he was right, I had put Kovis before him, because I wouldn't jeopardize his safety to appease Father's curiosity. But he'd never raged like this. Ever.

Phina, ever the quiet one, patted my thigh under the table. But her hand shook and thwarted the comfort she attempted.

I struggled to keep the tears that welled up from spilling over as servants brought the fourth course, hippocampus rangoon.

"Oh yes, cry like a child, Alissandra. You've certainly been behaving like a spoiled one."

I attempted a deep breath and failed, and as berry trifle, our dessert, appeared, I couldn't take any more. Proper decorum be damned. I threw my napkin on the table, and rose from my seat. I would not be attacked any longer for protecting my charge. I strode out of the room, my head held high, even though my heart was breaking from Father's words.

"Alissandra!" Father's bellow dogged me.

As soon as I reached the hall, I stopped fighting and surrendered to my raging emotions. My tears breeched the dam I'd barely held them behind, and I let them carry me and my pain with them.

No one would follow; they wouldn't dare, at least not right away with Father in this mood.

I flew down the hall clipping my wing on a corner when I came too close. The clatter of an overturned cart and shout of an upset servant chased after me. I didn't stop. I was so glad this family dinner was at our place; I could retreat to the sanctuary of my bedroom.

I reached the atrium. Above the fountains and abundant foliage, its clear dome revealed the gray hues of the early morning sky. Did it struggle and fight to hold onto this color and never let it fade? Did it fight to protect the night's treasures, those precious twinkling stars, that couldn't compete with the sun's brilliance? We all knew what would happen. It lost its battle every sun. Was I like this sky? Was the future inevitable? I couldn't let it be. I had to fight for Kovis like I'd been doing, no matter what Father did.

We were supposed to use the stairs. I didn't care. I swiped my cheeks as I launched and nearly collided with the pair of pure white caladrius flying about—they screeched their displeasure—one more party upset with me, whatever. I soared through the open space, up the three floors, Mema's correction sounding in my head even though she was still at dinner.

I beat my wings, slowing myself, then glided between the decorative, carved oak pillars and under the matching arch that connected them. I landed and crumpled into a heap on the white marble tile. Drawing my legs up and hugging them, I cradled my face. My chest heaved with sobs. Father had moved past withholding his love, past ignoring me, to raging mad at me.

He'd shouted that I'd brought this upon myself, among other unsavory remarks—my damn stubbornness, he'd called it. I'd gotten it from him so he only had himself to blame, but I'd never dare say that to his face. Father was famous for his dark moods, but he'd never been downright nasty, not like this morning with me… or any of my siblings. Not even close.

I couldn't do what Father asked of me, this was the fallout, and it was uglier than I could have ever anticipated.

I sobbed uncontrollably. I didn't care if any of the servants saw. Damn them. Damn him.

My chest started feeling looser as my angst flowed out, and at length, I sat up and took a deep breath, trying to rein in my emotions. My tears abated, and I wiped my face with the back of my hand.

Dinner hadn't yet ended judging by the silence. Just as well, I needed time to think, and while my brothers wouldn't come—they weren't the comforting types—I knew one or more of my sisters would find me.

I pushed up against the tapestry-covered wall and ambled down the hall to the bedroom I shared with my sister. I snorted. Mema would raise a brow, then frown at my "unmaidenly behavior." I snorted again for good measure and let out a soggy laugh.

The latch on the bedroom door opened easily, and I crossed the room and grabbed a hanky. As I blew my nose, I looked out the floor-to-ceiling window between my sister's and my bed. The sky had pinked, the gray again losing its battle with the sun as it peeked above the horizon. I took a deep breath trying to calm my emotions.

The sun wasn't a villain. It was just doing what it was supposed to do. It sent its first rays—warm, friendly rays—my way. Was it a sign from the Ancient One that he sided with me? Cared about me. I hoped it was and not their announcement that I should just do what Father said.

I settled my wings behind the headboard as I plopped down on the bed and nestled into the abundant pillows. I picked up my psaltery and started strumming a lullaby.

Music soothed me as much as it did my dream charges. It was like magic, maybe that's why I loved it so much. We didn't have magic in Dream realm, not like in Wake, and I loved the fact that singing or humming or strumming could lift my spirits like nothing else. It connected with my soul. And true to form, as the notes and chords and melody filled the room, my soul calmed on the notes.

Father and I had been at odds, but this morning's dinner... he'd drawn the family into the fray in the biggest verbal dressing down he'd ever delivered. It had been so scathing, so over the top. He'd never ever behaved that way with any of us.

He'd been absent on and off for most of my upbringing, no different than Mother, but my relationship with him had grown and blossomed the last few moons as we'd spent more time together. At least I thought it had.

So how could he treat me like this? Kovis was human. He was my charge for pity sakes. How could Father possibly think my love

● ● ●

for Kovis was greater than for him? I loved them both. Just differently.

My heart hurt.

Chapter Twenty

A knock at the door drew me from my thoughts.

"It's time we talk," Velma said as I opened it. She entered, and I peeked out in the hall wondering if more of my sisters were near, but saw no one. We'd see how long it took the rest of them to follow.

I joined Velma on my bed and met her eyes. "I... He's..."

Velma ignored my stuttering. "He calls you his 'favorite daughter' in private so the rest of us 'don't get jealous' doesn't he?"

My eyes grew large and my mouth dropped open. "How did you know?" I squeaked as my stomach clenched.

"You're not the only one he's told that." Matter-of-fact and to the point. That was Velma.

"Y... You, too?"

Velma frowned and then nodded.

"When?" I clutched the blankets tightly. It felt as if they alone anchored me.

"Do you remember way back when, when King Altairn was my dream charge?"

I nodded.

"I was happy to help Father see into the man's thoughts, and he started doting on me, like he has you. And yes, he called me his 'favorite daughter' as part of it." Velma scooted beside me and patted my arm.

I tried swallowing my shock, but it wouldn't go down. "What... What happened?" I bit my lip, trying to piece things together.

"No different than Delcina."

My eyes shot to hers.

"Yes, like Delcina, when King Altairn died, Father cast me aside even though I was his 'favorite' daughter and still mourning the man's loss. I got a new dream charge and he left me alone. It took some getting used to, but it was a relief in the end. But Father had shown me who he really was. So I've watched him and I try to protect my siblings as best I can."

Alarm bells clanged in my head. He used them?

"I feared he'd try something with you." I furrowed my brow as she continued. "Do you remember the festival of sandlings not long after your charge was born?"

I thought back. "You mean, the last time he was in an unusually good mood?"

Velma nodded. "The very one. He hasn't been happy since those provinces stopped him from retaking them."

I nodded. "Of course, Mother was there."

Velma raised a brow. "That may have been part of it, but I think he was also in a very good mood because he had just given you the child who would become crown prince, as your next charge."

My eyes went wide. "What? Wait."

Velma took a deep breath and bobbed her head.

I took a deep breath, and raised a hand to my neck. "What are you saying?"

Velma drew her lips into a line.

"You think Father is using me? Using Kovis? But why?" I met her eyes. "Why didn't you tell me before?"

"Would you have listened?" She raised a brow.

I closed my eyes and sighed.

"Every time I question Father's actions you downplay my concerns. Your view of Father is like Mother's, sunshine and rainbows. I doubted you'd believe me. And selfishly, I figured the longer you held onto that magic…. It's precious, Ali. And as long as your naiveté didn't hurt you…" Velma breathed out heavily.

I'd never thought about why Velma always opposed everything Father did or said. She never cut him slack. I'd never questioned why. It just was, but it made sense.

"It's okay, Ali."

She was right. I'd shut out all contrary opinions of Father. I should have opened my mind. If I had just listened, considered another perspective. Velma loved me, I had no concern about that, but I'd shut her down. I shook my head. Lesson learned. Never again. I'd force myself to listen, even if I expected to disagree.

"I'm so sorry," I said.

"I forgive you. You didn't understand, and I didn't give you reason to. I think I share equal blame." She straightened. "I know bits and pieces of what Father's done to you these last few moons, but would you tell me the whole story?"

I closed my eyes, my mind grappling to add what Velma had just shared into the mix. Before dinner, I'd felt completely and utterly alone. But it seemed Velma understood, she truly did. She'd experienced the same thing. I couldn't wrap my mind around it.

Moisture welled up as I locked gazes with her.

"Oh, little sister." She embraced me, rubbing my back.

I nodded into her shoulder. "Thank you." I hadn't cried this much in eons, but she didn't object. Her steady arms underscored her love for me and I started to believe things might be okay. She'd survived to tell about it. I would, too.

And so I told her my story.

When I finished, Velma blew out a breath. "What do you think he's really trying to do?"

My mind whirred trying to assemble a coherent theory. What would Father be able to do if he could tie several, even all, human thought threads together? It's what he'd been attempting, that and having me control Kovis's movements while he did.

If *I* could control several thought threads simultaneously, what could I do? My mind considered several scenarios. But I gasped as realization dawned. I would control them, not just their movements, but them. We'd gotten Kovis to do all sorts of things. I'd be able to control any human whose thought thread I held. I could make them do my will without question.

"Ali, what is it?" Velma grabbed my arms.

I tasted bile at the back of my throat.

If Father controlled humans, made them mindless beings who existed only to do his will... My breathing sped. "He wants to take over Wake."

"What?" Velma's pitch rose.

Father had been silent on our way back from Uncle Thao's after the autumn equinox gathering. Had Uncle given him the idea? Had he been mulling it over?

And if Wake fell, Dream would soon follow.

I didn't want to believe it. I'd trusted Father. Dyeus, please tell me no. I grabbed Velma's arms and squeezed back. The longer I thought about it. If it was true, his scheme went beyond the wildest mare I'd ever seen, and I'd seen plenty.

I tried to corral my raging thoughts, putting words to them as my mind continued galloping.

Father had been thwarted by the rogue regents he'd originally appointed. They'd prevented him from taking back the territory he believed he was rightfully entitled to. Twice. I'd seen the anger in his eyes when he'd returned most recently. I'd guessed he'd eventually try to retake them. But Wake?

My heart raced. That was a whole other horror.

Father knew me. He knew I'd resist his plan at some point. I'd started questioning his objective not long after the ball. And in the face of a barrage of questions, he'd asked just one, simple question. "Alissandra, do you remember our dance during Solstice?"

The emotion of Father's strong arms catching me, saving my life, had overwhelmed any further questions.

"Damn! Has all this been one huge scheme? Did he plan to use me to help him conquer Wake?" Even as I said it, I fought the notion. I swallowed hard trying to keep my stomach from emptying its contents.

"We have to stop him. He can't succeed. He can't." My voice sounded as hollow as my heart felt.

Velma shook me gently, just hard enough to regain my attention. "Oh, Ali, you've shouldered this all by yourself."

"I hadn't realized the full extent of it, but yes." I clenched my jaw. "I'll protect Kovis, all of Wake, if it comes to that."

Her grip tightened. "I know you will, and I'll help you."

We locked eyes, and I knew, in my soul, I was no longer alone with my burdens.

"Thank you." I felt exhausted. Father's overreaction at dinner had been because he'd been trying to use me, and I'd told him no. I now understood his rage.

Assuming Kovis and I were the only ones he was gaining proficiency with; we were the only ones who stood in the way of him taking over Wake. I'd thwarted him to protect my charge, but I'd unknowingly hindered Father's *grander* ambition. It all made so much sense.

"Do you suppose Father's exploiting Empress Rasa's sandman?"

"It's hard to say. Auden is her sandman if I remember correctly. I don't know him well. My guess is Father feels he can get away with more with his own daughter than a subject's son. He hasn't done anything to Alfreda, at least not that I've seen."

I exhaled. "That's a relief."

"You shepherd the crown prince's dreams. Alfreda's prince is the younger twin so he doesn't have as much influence."

"I hope you're right."

"You and me both, little sister, you and me both."

We sat in silence, coming to grips with Father's latest scheme.

● ● ●

Father loves us, doesn't he?" I held my breath waiting for her answer.

Velma smiled sadly. "I suppose he loves us all, in his own way."

She sighed. "Ali, it's clear to me from his actions that, in his mind, everything is really about him. It's why we don't all live together as a family, it's why he's never married Mother, it's why he only spends time with us when it's convenient for him. I could go on... I think he sees all of that, all of us, as... inconvenient."

My chest ached. "How... ?"

Velma rubbed my back. "I stopped asking ages ago. It's less painful that way."

I felt numb from her words, I loved Father, but Velma was right, everything had always been about him.

Silence dragged on as my mind came to grips with this... different reality, a reality I'd never once considered. Sunshine and rainbows... it hurt less, but it couldn't blunt the truth forever.

At length, Velma leaned back. "I'd wanted to talk to you privately, but there's another reason why I came before the others. In light of what you deduced, it hardly seems important—"

"How *did* you manage to leave dinner anyway?"

"I feigned needing to take care of a personal problem. Desperately."

I grinned.

"Anyway, we wanted to take you to the mushroom caves to cheer you up."

I brightened. It was only my most favorite spot on Lemnos. And it'd been much too long since my last visit. She was right, it did feel unimportant in this heartbeat, but Father wouldn't be able to advance his plans in my absence. And perhaps it might help me further put things in perspective.

"Who's coming?"

"All of us." Velma smiled. "Well, not Mema and Grandfather, but everyone else. Mema gave us her blessing."

I'd secretly hoped they'd support me, but I never expected this outpouring. All twenty-two of us... I couldn't remember the last time we'd gone on an outing together.

"How'd you have time to discuss and—"

Velma chuckled. "It's amazing what hand signals and passing napkins can do."

I laughed. "Oh, I love you all."

She grinned. "I need to change, and so do you. We'll meet in the atrium once everyone's ready."

I closed the door behind her and with it, my joy. My stomach twisted. Father planned to use me.

Part II: REM

Twinkle, Twinkle, Little Star

By Jane Taylor
Essex Wake Realm

Twinkle, twinkle, little star,
How I wonder what you are.
Up above the world so high,
Like a diamond in the sky.
Twinkle, twinkle, little star,
How I wonder what you are!

When the blazing sun is gone,
When he nothing shines upon,
Then you show your little light,
Twinkle, twinkle, all the night.
Twinkle, twinkle, little star,
How I wonder what you are!

Then the traveler in the dark,
Thanks you for your tiny spark;
He could not see which way to go,
If you did not twinkle so.
Twinkle, twinkle, little star,
How I wonder what you are!

Chapter Twenty-One

I'd barely finished changing when a knock came at my door. I cocked my head. I hadn't dallied. They couldn't be ready yet, could they?

Velma, Ailith, and Deor waited in their leather jackets and pants, flying boots, and gloves.

"How'd you get ready so quickly?" I asked, by way of greeting.

"Ready?" Velma asked, tone firm. A single word.

I wrinkled my brow. What had happened to her, after leaving me to put her in such a mood? I didn't ask. "Yeah, let me grab my gloves."

I threw my jacket over my head, my wings stopping it, and pulled it down. As we walked, I buttoned the bottom below where my feathers started. "Mother be blessed, Deor, do you have enough perfume on?" I fanned, emphasizing my point.

She shrugged. "Didn't have time to wash."

"What? In a moon? Who are you trying to impress? A little less next time, please, big sister."

She gave me a face but didn't reply.

"Don't make too much noise," Ailith warned. "Father's still here. Mema and Grandfather are keeping him occupied so we can slip you out."

The comment pained me, but I nodded. Yes, I wasn't prepared to see him, especially after what I'd deduced, and who knew what he'd do if he saw me. I finished buttoning the front placket of my jacket as we reached the last stair. I had my gloves on by the time we got to the entrance hall. Deor stood next to me and her perfume continued assaulting my senses. *Good grief.*

"Okay, everybody, listen up," Rankin said in a hushed tone. "We fly southeast so no one sees us. Once we're over the Palace of Sand, we'll adjust course. Got it? We males will protect you maidens should any threat come." He wagged his brows and ruffled his wings. Such a male.

Sandmaidens weren't allowed to train. Mema and others considered it unmaidenly and useless when there were so many trained males around. The thought always grated, like now. Most of my sisters and I didn't accept—I'm sure Bega, Eolande, and Eadu were content—but not the rest of us. We wanted to be treated equally. The males just laughed every time we told them that. They always responded that we didn't know what harsh training we were asking for. Harsh training or not, it had to beat needlepoint and sewing.

I tuned back in. Rankin finished by saying, "We've only got three guards, but we should be fine. Is everyone ready?"

Only three guards. Unheard of. We never left our place without at least twice that many. *Must just be this situation.* Well, that and probably because of the time of day. There shouldn't be any mares about—the beasts were nocturnal. I shuddered even thinking about the vile creatures.

I let the disturbing thoughts evaporate as we stepped outside and took off. Without any rest from the night's work, I felt a little sluggish and swallowed a yawn, but my spirits rose with the rising sun, and the weight of dinner's events lightened. Wasila flanked my left and Farfelee my right. I smiled at one, then the other, but neither seemed inclined to talk. Just as well, we probably were all still grappling with Father's verbal abuse directed at me. Deor flew directly ahead of me. How I wish she didn't. I'd have to make the best of it.

Leaving behind the white spires of home, it wasn't long before I glimpsed the bay. Like always, I could see through the clear, aqua water to the coral that littered the bottom—it made me think of a cauldron with so many colors mixing together.

"Oh, look." I pointed at a school of hippocampi swimming below. With the upper body of a horse and lower body of a fish, I loved watching these graceful creatures cut through the water—so swift and all in sync. Neither Wasila nor Farfelee reacted. *Odd.* Farfelee always enthused at seeing wildlife.

I thought I might have seen a mermaid not long after, but I didn't say anything because she ducked under an outcropping in the reef and I couldn't be sure. We weren't headed too far south, thank goodness, so I didn't expect to see any bunyip, fanged reptilian creatures, multiheaded sea serpents, or the fierce plesiosaur whose fins looked more like wings, gliding under water. These and other beings that I never wanted to meet face-to-face inhabited the dark depths of deeper waters.

Everyone was unusually quiet this morning. I glanced around. They all looked ahead. None of them joked or messed with each other. *Curious.* We all usually let loose on trips like this. Something felt off, but I couldn't put my finger on it. Father's behavior couldn't have affected them this much, could it?

"Palace of Sand," Rankin yelled from up front and our group shifted to an easterly path.

The tan spires of the sprawling palace complex rose from the horizon as we neared. Unlike most of our homes, this castle was constructed of sand. I could only guess it was because this was the nursery of crafted sand people—sandlings formed by Selova, the dream stitcher in our region of Father's realm—so it made sense that it would be made of sand.

Selova lived here and stitched together new sand people as the need arose. Humans had an expression when one of their kind passed on, ashes to ashes, dust to dust—it's what they were made of. Selova used sand to create these beings. Sand could be molded and shifted, and never broke down.

It would be a very long time before I had children of my own and I loved sandlings, so I went to the palace every now and again to get my baby fix. I think Selova enjoyed my company. She was a happy soul and easy to talk to, the consummate sand-grandmother. We'd chat about anything as I walked between the cradles, cooing at the babes or picking one up and playing with him or her. Sometimes I sang them lullabies. I always marveled—new immortal life. How she crafted them I'd never know, but she was a genius at it.

When she wasn't forming sandlings, she stitched dreams together, ensuring our charges slept through the night. One time, I asked her how she did it. She explained that she reached out with her mind to the dream canopy, much as we did as we began work each night. She'd wait and as one of us sprinkled sand in our charge's eyes to end a dream, she would grab the end of that dream with her mind and hold it until we'd found a new, relevant thought that needed working and gotten a dream going. Then she'd link the dreams together. Her work was critical to all of our success. I could always tell when she got overwhelmed with managing so many dreams because her response time slowed and invariably my charge would wake in the middle of the night.

The Palace of Sand was a small dot, and as we passed over, I saw a sled pulled by a team of sand cats. No doubt they were making a delivery to one of the outlying palaces. The musher smiled and waved. I waved back, but not one of my siblings so much as acknowledged him. Something was definitely up, my gut clenched, what was I missing?

Wynnfrith flew directly behind me. She hated it if I lagged when we flew in formation, as we were now. She'd smile, bat my feet, and tell me to stop daydreaming, as if I could dream.

I slowed.

She growled as my boots neared her face.

"Ha ha, that's funny Wynnfrith." I glanced over my shoulder. She wasn't smiling as I'd expected. Rather, she wore a scowl.

What? I ping-ponged my gaze between Wasila and Farfelee, then scanned the rest of my siblings. Not a sound from any of them. I bit my lip as my brain struggled to make sense of everything.

I barely held in a shriek as the pieces fell into place. *Oh Dyeus, no! Mares!* I flew in the middle of a pack of them. Their looks had fooled me. They'd transformed to look like my siblings. It's why no one acted normal. And Deor's perfume—it wasn't an accident she flew directly in front of me. It had masked their foul stench. Trained mares, only a few folks kept such creatures, Father being one. Had he sent them after me? They'd been in our palace, and he was the only one who had easy access.

My heart rate accelerated. I needed to stay calm. I closed my eyes and tried to take in a breath. They didn't know I knew. They hadn't ripped me apart. Yet. But how long would that last? I tried to look around slowly. I probably failed. There was no obvious escape, except down. I'd fly lower. But if I did, I'd give up the pretence of ignorance. But what choice did I have?

With my heart crawling up my throat, I dove... and they matched me wing beat for wing beat.

Imposter Wasila gave me a nasty look.

"What have you done with my family?" I struggled to keep my voice even.

Farfelee look-alike replied, "Nothing, they were not part of our orders."

Small mercy. I pivoted back to my left. "Where are you taking me?"

Wasila look-alike ran her, his, I didn't know, its eyes up and down me. I broke out in a cold sweat. I couldn't help it. "Rather demanding for someone in your position." It rolled its eyes. "You'll find out soon enough."

On the verge of panic, I pressed, "What do you intend to do to me?"

Farfelee-look-alike laughed and I pivoted back.

"We're under your father's orders. What do you suppose he ordered us to do with you?"

I sucked in a breath and searched the land we flew over. No one would hear me yell. There were no buildings of any kind. I wasn't paying attention and my wing clipped Mare-Farfelee, making it growl.

"Sorry. I'm sorry."

It showed off its long canines and I winced.

I needed to think, to bide my time until we got to... where? If we continued our course, we'd... *oh Dyeus, no!* We were headed toward the Palace of Time. What had Father told his mares to do?

Tremors shook my body, and it wasn't from the cold air we flew through. Small consolation, we weren't headed further south where family members lived who found entertainment in ripping humans apart in the most cruel and horrific of ways. Uncle Thao might be crazy, but at least he was peaceful. This other part of my extended family, not at all. No one ever invited these folks to holiday parties. The chaos that would have ensued would be unimaginable.

But my aunts, Nona, Ches, & Ta, who lived in the Palace of Time, while they didn't destroy humans in a violent manner, they measured the length of every human life and when it was over, they made sure it ended. They were renowned in both Dream and Wake. Despite my immortality, could they somehow alter my life? Is that what Father had tasked his mares with? Delivering me to them to make me see "reason." I wheezed. Or was this about Kovis? Father had been jealous of him. *Oh, Mother, no.* It made too much sense. "Show me you love me more than your charge." Father's challenge echoed in my ears. Would he try to eliminate Kovis? My gut told me as much. What could my aunts do to him? I gasped for air despite its plentiful supply. I had to get out of here. I dove again.

And my captors followed. Again.

"Let me go," I begged. I didn't care that I sounded pathetic. Father was pulling out all the stops when it came to Kovis.

Mare-Wasila smiled. "Those were not our orders."

"What were your orders?"
The mare only smiled.

Chapter Twenty-Two

I tried convincing myself that the Palace of Time was better than the alternative of my bloodthirsty relatives further south. I failed miserably.

Another branch of my family tree with bad fruit, these aunts—Grandfather's sisters—were reclusive crones as old as time itself, or so I'd been told. I'd never met them, never had occasion to, never wanted to. Everyone respected them, not out of admiration, but out of fear—fear of what they could do to the humans they cared about.

What would they do when we got there? We'd disturb them. *Damn!* The idea reeked of foolishness, and arriving unannounced, completely out of the question. We weren't asking for trouble, we begged for it. Maybe that's exactly what Father hoped. I crossed my arms and held myself but couldn't stop shaking.

The castle had not yet appeared when we flew into the first gray clouds. They were patchy at first, but grew denser the further we ventured. Fewer and fewer streaks of light penetrated the gloom until the sun abandoned its fight altogether, surrendering to the dark. I couldn't help but wonder if it was a sign. No, I couldn't allow my mind to wander there.

I'd been terrified since realizing mares had me surrounded, but the darkness added an ominous feeling. My stomach soured and made it hard to breathe as we flew on.

My mind raced. The more I thought about it, the more certain I became that this wasn't about me; it was about Kovis. I wanted to cry, to let out a whimper, but I couldn't indulge my weakness. I needed to be tough for Kovis. His life hung in the balance, and I needed a plan. How could I appeal to my aunts?

I'd be no good to my charge unless I could think and reason. I took several deep breaths and forced myself to let them out slowly. My mind slowed and I began mulling. I'd never approached a crone before. No doubt they'd jump all over me if I showed how scared I was—Kovis would be dead in a heartbeat. I needed to remain calm. But more, I needed to be confident. But what else? How would I convince them to leave him alone?

The thought fled as a towering edifice came into view against the backdrop of dark clouds. It looked nothing like the castles I was used to that spared height in favor of spreading their width across the ground like an overweight firedrake sleeping on its horde. This one was all height, and virtually no width. How it stood I'd no idea, but from a quick estimate it loomed no less than thirty floors tall. I took in the multitude of ornate spires that jutted from irregular, wart-like protrusions bulging from its sides. Spiky. All. The. Way. Up. To its pointy top. And creepy. Like boney fingers.

I swore I heard mournful music as we approached the shadowy courtyard, but only silence greeted us as we set down near the massive tree in the middle and surveyed our surroundings. The single, hulking door to the castle was unguarded. No surprise, you'd have to be a few notes short of a full measure to even consider threatening my aunts.

Mare-Rankin dispatched five of my mare-brothers to scout the premises. Once satisfied that nothing would harm us—as if that was likely with them being mares—the leader gave the command and every mare but he, shifted back into their wolf-like forms. I shrieked.

I couldn't help it. The shrill sound reverberated off the stones of the courtyard.

I was overwhelmed at the size of the beasts and the glow of their coats in the dim—they emitted a violet glimmer—had me scared out of my wits. Each mare came up to my chest. And the stench. I forced my stomach's contents back down as I stumbled forward trying to get out of the middle of their ranks. It had been one thing to realize they were mares, but small mercy, they'd been in nonthreatening forms. But this, no, absolutely not. I didn't have enough expletives to describe the depths of my loathing for these foul abominations. My aunts couldn't be worse than this. They couldn't.

I bumbled ahead and felt something on my face. I squealed again as I batted at whatever it was. The clear stuff clung to me and wrapped itself around the side of my head by the time I grabbed a strand and pulled it loose—a cobweb, one that hung between the giant tree's low branches and one of the spires. It wasn't life threatening. I tried to calm my breathing. I was okay. Everything was okay. Until a mare brushed against my back. I screeched again.

I beat my captors to the massive wooden door and stopped beneath the keystone where I panted. In the glow that these beasts' purple fur gave off, I could see rings in the wood. It seemed it was a slice of some enormous tree—more rings than any tree I'd ever seen and timeless to be sure. I looked but couldn't find a handle so I put my shoulder to the door and strained, but it didn't budge.

"Glad to see you're anxious to enter. Need some help?" Mare-Rankin asked. I'm sure my eyes were huge because the corner of the mare's mouth rose before motioning for me to step aside.

He didn't need to ask twice. I scrambled out of the recess of the door's frame and clutched the castle's stone front, making myself as small as I could as another mare stopped too close to me.

"Apor." The leader called one of his troops over, then bobbed his head toward the obstacle. "Open the door for us."

A heartbeat later, the door's hinges creaked in protest, but granted us admittance. Mare-Rankin motioned the brut back from the black entry and said, "After you, princess."

The too-close mare didn't move and I was forced to squeeze between it and the rough stone, leaving some skin and several feathers behind before reaching the door. I inhaled deeply as soon as I crossed the threshold. Unpolluted air.

But my steps stirred up the layer of thick dust and I started sneezing. The leader laughed. "Prefer this to our scent?"

I scowled, although it probably wasn't very convincing between a multitude of sneezes. I covered my nose with an elbow to force myself to stop. It seemed no one had been here in a very long time, until I spotted a trail of Father-size footprints in the dust. A pair of winding staircases met not far ahead. The prints headed up the left one.

"Come on." Mare-Rankin motioned me to follow him, toward the same staircase Father had climbed. With my arm still over my face, I scurried after, ahead of his pack. But I felt their hot breath on my wings. Twenty-five ginormous creatures who'd probably rather be doing something beastly, than escorting me. The thought of flying flitted through my mind, but I knew it would be suicide in the dim and unfamiliar place.

My aunts. The thought broke through the horror that consumed me. I would see them in mere heartbeats. I shuttered. I needed to calm down before we got there.

We reached a landing and mounted the next flight of stairs that clutched the rounded walls.

I needed to be composed and confident to fight for Kovis, I reminded myself.

Up we climbed. I never thought I'd be grateful to take on so many stairs. One, two, three—on I counted, trying to calm my racing thoughts with each step. Not a wonder my aunts never ventured from here. I'd stay put, too, if I had to go through all this to leave the place. I started panting.

Father didn't know my charge, not at all, but there was no way he had anything good to say about him. Kovis's future depended on me and I wouldn't let him down.

At long last, we reached the top and Mare-Rankin waited for the pack to assemble before proceeding into a hallway that was only dimly lit from a row of windows to the left.

I'd paint Kovis in the most positive light possible no matter what question my aunts asked, assuming they asked me questions. Surely that's what I was here for, wasn't it? I pushed the worry aside. Yes, if I could help my aunts see all Kovis's positives and minimize his negatives, help them understand why I cared so deeply for him, surely, they'd understand that he deserved to live. My mouth went dry. It wasn't much of a plan, but it was a plan. It was. A teeny, tiny speck of confidence took root. Hopefully it would be enough. Now to just be convincing.

We stopped as we reached the first beings we encountered, a pair of black-robed stewards. They bore no weaponry so they would be little challenge for the brutes following me. They stood, one on either side of a set of open doors from which artificial light and all manner of low mechanical noises emanated.

My aunts were just ahead. These two were the only beings standing between me and them. I swallowed... hard. A flush of heat consumed me and my hands grew clammy.

Chapter Twenty-Three

The pair of stewards looked up and scanned our party. The one on the right said, "You must be the princess. We've been expecting you."

They were expecting me. I willed my fingers to stop twitching, without success.

The other attendant raised a brow and gave us an evil eye. "Don't touch anything."

"Come." The first steward turned and without looking back, strode into the torch-lit chamber, his black robes swishing behind his onyx wings.

Other than the dread of meeting my powerful crone aunts, I didn't know what to expect when I'd found out we were headed to the Palace of Time, but what I saw hadn't entered my mind: The smell of incense greeted us, and then the low sounds of ticking, metal balls rolling across metal, tinkling water, chimes, and more. They joined to create a melody as we followed our guide between rows of ancient shelves, which stretched floor to ceiling, crammed with all manner of time-keeping devices.

Tan-robed attendants flitted between a sea of clear hourglasses, tipping them over just before the sand ran out, while other stewards monitored elaborate contraptions with dripping water and added more to some. Another section of shelves with robed custodians scurrying up and down movable ladders had devices in which a metal ball rolled down a zigzagging track to move the hands on a timepiece. A simpler measuring device that we came upon looked to be nothing more than candles burning. A steward would change out a melted flambeau when the wick guttered. Some candles looked to be perilously close to expiring. I hated to think what happened if a candle wasn't tended to expeditiously.

So many different devices. My feeling of dread gave way to awe.

"Please keep up," the steward warned.

He jarred me from my reverie, and the reality of the situation reasserted itself. I felt the warm breath of the beasts following on my wings and heard their nails clicking on the stone floor. Mare-Rankin strode beside me, a stern expression making the muscles in his jaw bulge. I clutched my stomach and averted my eyes to the back of our guide's worn robe.

After passing several more shelves brimming with devices, ladders, and attendants, our guide stopped and I peered around him. My aunts, Nona, Ches, and Ta, sat on a dais, hunched in rocking chairs, conversing. Fear and awe overwhelmed me and I gripped my jacket buttons.

They seemed oblivious to our presence. Or maybe they were hard of hearing. I took the time to study them. Their stringy, white hair fell over plain gray-robed shoulders. Nothing but the fact that they were older than time itself boasted anything remarkable about them. But no matter how unassuming they seemed, everyone feared them, and I was smart enough to tremble.

"Pardon me, Moirai," our guide interrupted, then bowed.

I followed his lead and went down on one knee as well. With my brow a hairsbreadth from the floor, a shrill voice chastised, "You think yourselves equal?" I couldn't tell if she addressed me staring at the floor as I was.

"No Moirai, we meant no disrespect." Mare-Rankin stumbled over his words and, from my periphery, I felt the breeze caused by the flutter of wings and caught a gray robe swish. Rankin crumpled into a bow. The crone might be old but she had speed. All breathing noises, all noises actually, that had been emanating from behind me, ceased. What had she done to them?

Shuffling feet approached me and I swallowed, praying she didn't do anything to me. I felt thick fabric swish to a stop on the top of my head.

"Alissandra, rise child."

Like a tortoise peeking from its shell, I lifted my head and my gaze traveled up the crone's robe, past hands hidden in the robe's overlong sleeves, until I was forced to sit back on my heels to take in her face. Beside her olive-colored skin and flat, broad nose, she had dark circles under her eyes and enough wrinkles to resemble a leathery, shriveled up fruit. But her eyes... they were alive. The hazel centers were greener than any eyes I'd seen before, and they pierced me. I inhaled sharply.

A corner of her mouth hitched up as she turned and retreated to her chair at the left of her sisters. Mare-Rankin maintained his hunched posture as I awaited instruction. I didn't know if he couldn't move or was choosing not to for fear of more consequences. I presumed nothing. The last thing I wanted was Kovis's life cut short because of perceived disrespect. My aunts may be old, but if this one was any indication, I understood how they'd achieved their reputation. They were forces to be reckoned with.

I bit my lip before I reminded myself to be calm and be confident.

"Rise and approach, maiden." The middle crone motioned me forward with her bony, bent claw of a hand.

My gaze remained locked on her as I pushed up and compelled myself forward on quivering legs. Stay calm, I again reminded myself. Easier said than done.

They were definitely sisters, the similarities were too many to mistake. Their eyes, despite being different colors, probed and scrutinized everything, missing nothing.

I stopped when the middle crone bobbed her head. I guessed that's what she'd meant. I wasn't sure.

"Why are you here?" my aunt, the one to her right, asked.

Because these monsters abducted me to accomplish my father's business? I couldn't say that. "To be honest, I'm not sure."

"Honesty is a virtue. You'll find not much else will serve you here," she replied in a sharp tone, then nodded again. I took it as a sign for me to continue.

I swallowed. They wouldn't care about the trip to the mushroom caves my siblings and I had planned that wasn't going to happen. "My"—how to describe them—"escorts… would not reveal… I believe my father approached you about my dream charge, Prince Kovis Altairn."

Another nod. This time from the rightmost crone. "Indeed he did."

My middle aunt explained, "Your father approached us and made a request to modify your charge's lifespan. We wanted to hear the other side of the story before taking action, or not."

I resisted the urge to rub my arms.

The crone on the left interrupted my worrying. "*I* decide the length of every human's life." My mind whirled. From what I knew of the three, that would make this my Great Aunt Ches. "When a child is born, your Aunt Nona sets in motion a new device, one corresponding to the time-keeping customs of a particular region." The middle sister nodded. So that's why there were so many different types of timepieces. She continued, "Your Aunt Ta stops an apparatus when an individual has exhausted the suns I've allotted him or her." My rightmost aunt smiled.

A chill went up my back. So I needed to appeal to both Great Aunt Ches to not alter Kovis's lifespan and especially make Aunt Ta see reason not to cut his life short, without offending Aunt Nona, if Kovis was to be saved. My stomach tightened. I'd never been good at playing political games. In fact, I sucked at it. My sisters teased that they could read me without much effort—yes, my naivety had had its drawbacks at times.

"Your charge is twenty-five," Aunt Ches said. A statement. "I set his life to end on—"

I inhaled as Aunt Nona cleared her throat and gave Ches a stern look.

"Fine, I won't say how long I gave him." She smoothed her robe as I exhaled. I didn't know if I wanted to know. Despite the inevitability of it, it was always painful when I lost a charge. I couldn't help but grow attached. "You'll understand there are far too many humans to keep track of the intimate details of how well or poorly any one of them use those suns."

I nodded; it was the safest option of responses I could give.

"Get to the point," Ta cut her sister short. Ches frowned as Ta took over, "Let's review his past."

Crap. His past. They wanted to go there right away. I had a strategy, I reminded myself. His history had made Kovis who he was. He'd started out happy but after his father had… I despised thinking about what his father had done. It was despicable. Between that, and Dierna—the thought of her made me fume—Kovis had grown cold, shut down, and despairing more times than not, of late. Kovis and his siblings never talked about the former. He avoided thinking about the later. I didn't blame him. I wondered, had my aunts had anything to do with it? I raised a hand.

Aunt Nona nodded.

"May I ask a question?"

"You may ask, but we make no promise to answer."

My throat constricted. "Do… do you have any say in what happens in a human's life?"

The three sisters ricocheted glances. It seemed they had an unspoken language all their own, much like Kovis and his twin when they were little—they'd driven their nannies crazy with it. At length, each of the trio nodded. Would I get an answer?

Ches said, "No dear, we do not control what happens to a human during their lifetime. The human mind is far more inventive than are we. Why, they make life so much more exciting for themselves, and each other, than we could. We could not compete. An accident out of stupidity or a casualty out of malice, there are so many ways a human can die before the number of suns I've allotted. Really, it's quite amazing there are any of them left what with their ambitions and greed."

Could humans die before the length of life my aunts granted? I covered my mouth. Is that what had happened to Drake and the other dream charges I'd had who'd died young? Had an accident, and not my aunts, ended their lives too early? The thought eased some of my angst toward my aunts, although my young charges deaths still felt meaningless.

"But back to the topic at hand," Aunt Ta said, drawing my attention back.

If nothing else, she was direct and focused. I resisted the urge to slouch. I hoped I could convey to them who Kovis had been. I knew my aunts would love that picture of him.

I could bargain from that position, couldn't I? I had to, because how long Kovis lived rested squarely on my shoulders, and I felt the weight press.

Chapter Twenty-Four

"Tell us how you came to be assigned this dream charge," Aunt Nona asked. There was no humor in her tone.

I exhaled and looked up at the ceiling. I loved this question. It was nothing dark. How to have all their questions be like this one?

I told them about losing Drake and having the opportunity, before my mourning moon was even over, of being assigned a twin. And not only a twin, but a prince.

All three of my aunts sat with their hands folded on their laps throughout my telling, never interrupting, just letting me talk.

I'd noticed their quiet, but I'd been so focused on telling my story that it hadn't unnerved me, like in these heartbeats as their silence dragged on.

I turned my attention and listened behind me never daring to look at my captors lest I somehow offend my aunts. I heard only silence. Mare-Rankin must still be kneeling and his sidekicks frozen, good. They deserved what they got.

My aunts each seemed to be mulling over what I'd shared. Mulling and mulling and mulling. What could they possibly glean from it or question? Tell me I hadn't doomed Kovis at the outset. *Oh Dyeus, please, no.*

My heart sped as they took to exchanging looks once more.

After what felt like an eternity, Aunt Ches finally broke the silence. "Tell us two significant early memories you have of your dream charge."

What had their silent conversation concluded? Certainly they had to have decided something or they wouldn't be asking another question, right? I felt my knees start to buckle, but kept myself up.

Why would *two significant, early* memories matter relative to assessing Kovis's life over the last twenty-five annums? He'd been an infant and without choice. I didn't know, but if that's what they wanted, I'd oblige—it beat trying to hedge my way around one of many not so positive events in his life.

I pondered what to share and stopped as a particularly fond memory came to the fore.

I'd never told anyone my deep down feelings about Kovis. I rarely admitted them to myself. They couldn't know either, aunts or no. So I carefully schooled my features as I began the tale.

"Alfreda and I were both tired. Dark circles marred the flesh below our eyes. We'd taken to spending most of our time together, in either of our rooms, until we got through the first stage with our twin charges. I was so glad we had each other.

"'Hey, do you hear that?' I remember Alfreda asking."

Aunt Ches tilted her head.

"'A hum. It's new. Yeah, one of our twins is making some sort of humming sound. Listen,' she'd said.

"I remember closing my eyes and focusing. And I finally heard the strange notes. It was a slow vibration of sorts coming from Kovis, although he hadn't yet been named.

"I'd never heard anything like this hum but... I didn't know, perhaps all twins hummed. I realized Alfreda's twin didn't, but that was beside the point. I wondered if maybe the sound would go away once he emerged into the world. It wasn't his fault that none of my other charges had been talented enough to exhibit it. He was just extraordinarily gifted, that's all."

Aunt Nona chuckled.

I went on, "Turns out, it didn't go away, but only intensified as he grew. It got downright loud, as it's been ever since, when his powers finally manifested, but that was the start of it."

"So he's a powerful mage," Ches said.

"I presume so although I've no way of knowing how he compares with others."

Nona nodded. "Any explanation why you heard it with him and none of your previous charges?"

"Sorry, no." I drew my lips into a line.

"And your second significant early memory of this charge?" Aunt Ta asked.

I nodded.

"Rasa, Kovis's sister, was two at the time. She was always the doting big sister, smothering her brothers with kisses. She loved making them laugh. She also loved playing teatime and with her brothers who were only seven moons old, as they made the perfect guests.

"Well, Nanny Leida sat Kovis on the rug beside Kennan and then handed Rasa a small mirror. She pretended to primp her hair with one hand as she held the glass in the other. "'Aren't I a beautiful princess?'"

A corner of Aunt Nona's mouth rose as I embellished the tone of Rasa's voice.

"Kovis gnawed on a toy and drooled, watching her."

I barely suppressed a chuckle. He'd been so sweet as a babe.

"'You must look your best for my tea,' Rasa said and she came around behind Kovis and held the mirror before him, proceeding to pretend comb what little of his dark-brown hair there was. And I gasped. It was the first time I'd seen his face."

My heart sped even now.

"His eyes. They were so beautiful. Royal blue with hazel centers. I'd never seen eyes like his."

I couldn't help smiling.

"Rasa passed the mirror to Kennan and when he held it up…"

I drew a hand to my chest. The moment had seared itself into my memory.

"I realized Kovis and Kennan looked *exactly* alike. They weren't just twins, they were *identical*, well except Kennan's eyes which are russet like tea that's steeped too long."

I bit back a smile trying not to give away anything more of my feelings for my charge.

"So he was handsome even at that age." Aunt Ta said.

I nodded. "They both were. But it was more than that. I marveled at the fact that… they looked *identical*. I didn't understand how it was possible for two separate human beings to look the same. It's incredible. As if the Ancient One liked the look so much that he decided to do it again."

Nona chuckled.

Aunt Ta stood and wandered down the steps toward me. What was she doing?

I furrowed my brow as she passed me by. All that and this was how my aunts responded?

I pushed the thoughts aside, was I supposed to follow? I took a chance and did. A tan-robed attendant joined us as we wandered among the shelves and Ta pointed at several timekeeping mechanisms and gestured at others, instructing in a low murmur, while the attendant scribbled notes. We approached a mechanical device in which a ball rolled. Aunt Ta blew away the dust that had collected. "Polish it until you can see your reflection in the brass."

The attendant nodded then hurried away, presumably to get supplies to do so.

"This one still has a long life before him. We must keep his device spit spat clean."

I nodded, unsure why she'd told me.

"Nona didn't think we should tell you, but no doubt you'd enjoy seeing your charge's device."

"You'd show me?" My throat felt as if a serpent had wrapped itself around my neck and squeezed.

"How would that make you feel to know the end of his days? To know when you'll be rid of this one and getting your next charge?"

My mouth dried as Aunt Ta's comment struck me, no different than if Dyeus had hit me with a celestial bolt. How could she say that? I loved my charges. I never wanted their suns to end. "Thank you, but no. I don't want to know."

"Interesting," she said under her breath. "Wise beyond your time."

What was that supposed to mean? Had that been a test? Had I passed it? Failed it? What? How might my response affect Kovis?

She said nothing more as I followed her meandering path back through the menagerie of shelves. Mare-Rankin hadn't moved—he still bowed and his compatriots stood stiffly, just the way we'd left them.

"You may rise," Aunt Ta commanded as we reached the front of their midst. I couldn't help but gloat at the treatment they'd received. Not when they'd done what they had to me.

Groans and grunts echoed about the hall—from Rankin in particular who'd been stuck in a most awkward position—as Aunt Ta mounted the steps and sat back down in her rocker.

"We're the ones who should be groaning, not you young things," Aunt Ches scolded. Her comment silenced all further sounds.

Aunt Ta leaned in and her sisters bent forward. In a hush, I could only hear snippets of, it seemed she relayed what she'd learned from our little excursion among the shelves. My stomach twisted. It *had* been a test. Had I passed or failed?

They finally sat back and Aunt Ches said, "So you took a liking to your charge almost immediately. You think he's special. It's what your Father claimed, too. Very well, we'll keep that in mind."

My breath hitched. "Keep it in mind?" Father probably hadn't bothered to tell them *he'd* made Kovis come between us.

"Of course, you'll paint every response in what you consider the most favorable light."

I inhaled sharply. They hadn't cared about the memories, they'd wanted to see how I recounted them. I'd been so stupid. And now they knew how I felt about Kovis, or at least in part. Stupid. Stupid. Stupid.

"This is as much about you as it is your charge."

"Really? May I ask why?"

"All shall be revealed in due time." It wasn't an answer.

Aunt Ta looked beyond me and gave a nod. I turned as an attendant bobbed her head, then reached out and turned a sand timer on its side, stilling it. I gasped. Had she…? It felt like a rock thudded in the pit of my stomach. She'd just ended a human life. Was it Kovis's?

Please don't be Kovis. Please don't be Kovis. I couldn't have screwed this up so easily, could I? My heart raced.

No. It couldn't be him. I couldn't have ended him. No. It had to have been another. It had to have.

My panic over what I had just witnessed was overtaking my thoughts, Aunt Ta had just killed someone's charge without so much as a flicker in her eyes.

I held myself, wanting to deny what I'd seen. Had the timing been a coincidence? Surely my aunts weren't threatening me, as I now knew Father had upon occasion. Were they making sure I knew where I stood, or more correctly, where Kovis stood? Would they do that?

My stomach clenched. Was I, was Kovis, a piece in some political game, caught between them and Father?

I took a deep breath, realizing it didn't really matter: the nod of Aunt Ta's head is all it would take for a human to perish. And they knew my strategy. *Shred my wings!*

Had they just ended Kovis's life?

Chapter Twenty-Five

"Come with us." Ta stood up, along with her sisters, and motioned me forward with an open palm.

I didn't want to go anywhere with them. Not when it might have been Kovis they ended.

A rumble rose behind me. I glanced over my shoulder to see the mares prowl forward. "Excuse me," Mare-Rankin cleared his throat. "We were given explicit orders not to let her out of our sight." I almost wanted him to get his way. Almost.

My aunts didn't say a word, only locked eyes with my captor while his cronies surrounded him, growling their support of their leader.

Aunt Ta spoke, "Rather bold aren't you. Would you like me to pause time for you once more? It's no problem, really."

Rankin huffed and looked to the ceiling. They'd certainly put him in his place. If fear of where they planned to take me hadn't turned my stomach into a rock, I would have smirked and maybe even made a rude gesture.

I let my aunts lead me to the right of the dais. I tried to discretely wipe my sweaty palms on my leather pants—it didn't do much good—but Aunt Ta saw and raised a corner of her mouth. Aunt Ches disappeared through the door or whatever you called what covered the circular opening—it swirled in a host of dull colors. What was I getting myself into? I stretched out a hand but felt nothing.

Aunt Nona smiled beside me. "It won't bite."

I drew in a breath and held it as I stepped through, then drew a hand to my mouth as I took in the room that lay before me. An expansive floor to ceiling window filled virtually the entire far wall with the clear, blue sea. How was it not the gloomy clouds? I'd no idea and I feared to ask. But the room felt homey with a huge crackling fireplace to the left, before which had been arranged three sofas with a short, wood table in the middle. Colorful rugs were scattered about. Every appointment was simple and lacked ostentation.

"No, that was not your charge's life Ta just ended," Nona said as she knotted a bright yellow belt that coordinated with the bold flower print of her orange robe about her waist.

My heart surged with relief. Kovis was safe. He was safe. I exhaled. Her assurance made me appreciate that she wore bright colors, more than I should have.

"I love your robe!" I exclaimed. I often wished we could wear our solstice ball gowns all the time—it looked like my aunts had had the same idea, but they'd done something about it.

She looked over and nodded as a corner of her mouth hitched.

Ches had removed her sandals and opted to go barefoot, as I saw when she stepped over to one of the divans. She finger-combed her white hair and pulled it back into a leather stick barrette with a butterfly design. "That's better," she declared, sitting.

A steward offered her a beverage.

"Make yourself comfortable, Alissandra," Aunt Ta encouraged as an attendant helped her remove her gray robe from around her black wings. Underneath, she wore a red-velvet, ankle-length vest overtop a long sleeved, white-linen top with gathered neck. She pulled a purple robe from another hook on the wall.

● ● ●

142

I felt inappropriately dressed in my leather flying jacket and pants, but my aunts didn't comment as I took a seat on the left divan and settled my wings over the back, across from Aunt Ches.

"Not quite what you expected?" Nona chuckled as she buttoned her grass green robe, picked up some sort of mechanical contraption from a workbench, and joined us. She began to spin the toothed wheels as she sat. Ta gave her a stern look. "Sorry." She silenced the thing.

A steward stopped in front of me. "Would you care for something to eat or drink?"

My stomach rumbled. I hadn't eaten much of anything at dinner. I looked around at my aunts. Was this another test? Was this what this whole encounter was?

"Anything you'd like, just name it," Aunt Nona said, fingering her device.

Aunt Nona was right. I hadn't expected any of this. It seemed they wanted me to feel at home, but why? So I'd spill every one of Kovis's secrets? So it'd be crystal clear how I felt about him? Never. Who knew what they might do with such information.

Before this morning's events, I probably would have blindly trusted they meant Kovis no harm. It's what I'd always believed about Father. He'd probably told them as much about me—I was too trusting and easily deceived. No more, at least if I could help it. My aunts had discerned my strategy, but I wasn't done fighting for my Dreambeam.

What to do? I suppressed a smile when an idea popped into my head. Perhaps two, or in this case four, could play this game. They tried to assess whether they would modify the length of Kovis's life by understanding how he'd lived—I presumed if he didn't measure up, they'd grant Father's request. Kovis wasn't the most socially attractive human at present, and I'd been concerned. But who said I had to tell them actual events? What could I dream up? How could I combine enough truth with positive stories to convince them to leave Kovis alone? I'd fantasized about Kovis enough; perhaps I could weave a few details from those into my tales. It'd surely make them upbeat. Aunt Ta's comment about honesty being a virtue and not much else serving me here, bounced around my brain, but I ignored it.

With another plan in place, I smirked. What outlandish dish could I ask for? "Breakfast is my favorite meal. In fact, I could eat breakfast food all night, every night if I got the chance."

Aunt Ta smiled.

"If it's not too much trouble, I'd *love* some fairy dust pancakes with bubblefruit syrup and dragon horn tea." Only the rarest of ingredients, I knew fairy dust was virtually impossible to get. And dragon horn? Out of the question. First of all, dragons weren't common around these parts. And second, someone had to be very courageous to harvest a horn from a living, fire-breathing beast. If they came up with decent dishes, I might reconsider trusting them, but until then... we'd see.

"You love fairy dust pancakes, too?" Ches grinned. "I'm the only one of my sisters who does. It's nearly impossible to get fairy dust at times. You have good taste."

Aunt Ta forced a smile. So did I. Was she kidding? I couldn't tell. But what were the odds?

"So, where were we?" Aunt Ta said.

"Ta, let the poor thing eat before more questions. Surely you heard her stomach complain," Ches interrupted.

Ta raised her hands in surrender. "Fine."

"While we wait"—Aunt Nona's face lit up—"would you like to see the latest time keeping device I'm working on?"

I turned my head between Ches and Ta. Neither objected so I stood. "I'd love to."

She led me over to a workbench against the far wall. "Have a seat."

I sat down on the other stool as she lit several candles, then proceeded to explain the intricacies of the apparatus before us.

She'd somehow figured out that a sun could be divided into equal periods, each of which she called hours, and so on, and so on, and so on. The mechanical device somehow kept pace with all of her calculations. I got lost as she explained it, but she seemed committed to her idea and convinced that it would make measuring a human's life that much more precise, something I was all in favor of.

My breakfast's arrival saved me from more explanation and I eagerly retreated to the sofas. Aunt Nona didn't seem to notice I'd left for I kept hearing her talk to herself as she tinkered, lost in her own world.

Aunt Ches patted a spot next to her and chuckled. "Don't mind her. She's very enthusiastic about making sure every human gets each and every breath I allot them."

I forced a smile, thinking of the life she'd snuffed out. Now to get them to care about permitting Kovis every heartbeat of time she'd allotted him at birth.

I leaned forward and poured bubblefruit syrup over the stack of fairy dust pancakes, then passed the flask to Aunt Ches who had ordered her own stack. My first bite... *Oh, sand.* I thrust a hand up— I'd have vexed Mema to no end if she'd seen me. I swallowed. "These are the best tasting fairy dust pancakes I've *ever* had."

Ches grinned. "Not a bad batch, although Cook's made better."

"Better?" I croaked. "I didn't know that was possible."

"It's all in the freshness of the ingredients," Ta explained.

Clearly. Not a wonder these crones still had a twinkle in their eyes and spunk after all this time despite their haggard appearances. Although color certainly softened their looks and made them look a bit younger, too.

I took a sip of my dragon horn tea. *Mmm.* That was tasty, too. Maybe I would moderate my plan... Umm, no, Kovis's life was still on the line.

"Shall we continue?" Aunt Ta asked, taking a sip of a dragon fruit cocktail that closely matched her robe. "Nona, please join us."

"Nona!" Aunt Ches echoed several heartbeats later when my aunt still hadn't responded.

"Huh? What? Oh, sorry. Coming." She took another dragon fruit cocktail that a steward handed her as she sat. She sputtered on the first sip and wrinkled her face. "Tart."

I hid a smirk, taking another sip of my tea.

* * *

"Now that everyone's appetite is satisfied, let's continue. Alissandra has things to do besides yammer at us until the sun sets," Aunt Ta grumped.

I let a corner of my mouth rise. But I knew she was about to pose the next question and my hand found the back of my neck.

"How a human behaves at a young age reveals much about him and who he will become. What was your charge like as a youngster? Give us a few notable examples."

It wasn't an undesirable question, and I thought for some time, at length selecting two. "I have a couple examples that I think will help. This first one is when Kovis was two.

"The nannies had taken Rasa, Kennan, and Kovis to the stables 'to see the horsies.'"

I smiled, remembering. It was so sweet.

"Despite the fact that the animal dwarfed him, its head half his size, he hadn't shied away. Rather Kovis petted the sleek fur with enthusiasm, even babbling to the animal.

"And when they held him atop the chestnut mare, he clapped and giggled. Kennan shrieked in terror when it came his turn despite Rasa's calming words.

"Well, as you might guess, the horse startled, ending the outing."

"So your charge, at the tender age of two, showed he's not intimidated by what he doesn't yet know or understand," Aunt Nona summarized, before I could.

My mouth dropped open. "Ye... yes, exactly." She was old, but she was quick.

Aunts Ta and Ches bobbed their heads awaiting my next tale so I moved on. The events flooded my mind.

"The nannies took the children into the capital city of Veritas one sun. They hadn't gotten far when Kovis spotted Master Barin, their favorite storyteller, and begged to go listen. So they did.

"The man shifted in a well-worn, stuffed leather chair. A basket with coins sat near his feet for grateful listeners to contribute to. He clapped and beamed when he set eyes on the children, then bowed. Kovis asked him to tell them a story about their father.

"Master Barin chuckled as he settled back in the chair and stroked his long, gray beard, as he gathered his thoughts."

I drew my hands to my chest, remembering.

"The children joined the dozen and more children and parents, scooting close and a hush fell as they waited. At length, the old man surveyed his congregation of hopeful faces and nested himself more comfortably. 'Once upon a time, in a land far, far away, but not unlike our very own, there lived a dragon...'

"I had no doubt Kovis's eyes grew wide through the telling, his siblings' eyes surely had.

"Master Barin likened the emperor to a kind, but fearsome dragon who, unlike most firedrakes, shared of his horde for the betterment of all in its territory. This particular adventure focused on bad men who attacked and tried to steal from the creature."

I beamed at the cuteness of it all.

"The tale frightened Kovis even though he wouldn't admit it under Rasa's probing on their way back. I knew I would need to calm Kovis's mind and help him rationalize the threat. But as I started pulling the disparate threads of Kovis's memory together as he slept, I stopped.

"'I'm that nice dragon,' Kovis said to Kennan, thumping a hand on his chest. 'I made those bad men give me back my stuff. Then I made them help the good people of the land.'"

"He'd processed his fear without my help. I was seriously impressed."

I turned to see Aunt Nona take a sip of her beverage and Ches motion the steward to clear her dishes. Had they listened?

Ta sat bobbing her head, rubbing a finger over her upper lip. "Not being intimidated by what he doesn't yet know or understand and rationalizing what frightens him. Very useful talents for a leader."

"Leader? Are you saying something's going to happen to his family to make him...?" My stomach churned.

"Yes, indeed, very useful." Aunt Nona ignored my question and spun the notched wheel. It whirred at a high pitch.

Ches frowned, but Nona seemed lost in thought.

"What are you saying? Why is that important?" I asked.

"Don't get any ideas. We are not disclosing his future to you. It's only helpful should he become emperor one day."

"But you know if he will, don't you?"

Aunt Ta cut in. "It sounds like he's got vision and fight in him, too, what with reforming those men."

"Of course, if put to the wrong end, it could just as easily create problems," Aunt Ches mused.

My aunts nodded.

What problems might be created if he didn't fear the unknown? Or if he fought for a cause he believed in? Visions of grandeur like Father? I shuddered. No, Kovis wasn't like that. Nor was he like *his* father, for that matter. *Dyeus, no.*

I hadn't embellished these two stories, hadn't thought I needed to, and my aunts had read into them a whole lot more than I ever had.

An empty feeling filled the pit of my stomach. What might I inadvertently reveal to them about Kovis as they asked more questions? I was his only hope, yet I might well doom him.

Chapter Twenty-Six

"Pardon me." The steward who had served my breakfast stopped behind me. "I'm sorry to interrupt, but a human is about to be born."

I'd seen them snuff out a life, what would they do when new life entered Wake realm?

"Thank you, Ancel," Aunt Ches replied.

"If you'll excuse us," Aunt Ta said, looking me in the eye.

"We won't be long," Nona added.

"Oh, of course." I got up and wandered over to an open door at the back of the room—a normal wooden door—and peeked in to see a host of shelves much like the ones the time pieces sat on, but these were crammed full of books from floor to ceiling.

Would they mind me looking at their collection? I looked over my shoulder. They hunched together no doubt discussing how long a life they would grant the babe—I prayed it was long and peaceful.

I raised a hand. "Excuse me."

I got no response from any of them, so I decided to take a chance. I ran a hand along the first shelf, reading the titles: *Glorian and Githa: Tragedy of Star-crossed Lovers, Gone with the Breeze, Ego and Enmity, Feel and Feeling*. I recognized the titles as being romances. I was surprised since I thought my aunts stayed put for the most part, but clearly, they had some way of procuring them. The next shelf continued with more romance titles. I felt my face warm as the titles got spicier. Whew, maybe I should find a different sex... section. I fanned myself and moved to a shelf *way* on the other side of the room. Nope, more of the same. I gulped. This was one huge library filled with nothing but... from eons past... Did the scrolls I'd spotted also... Surely, they had a music or lullaby section, something, anything else. I scanned more titles. No. I beat a hasty retreat, feeling warm. And I hadn't even opened a book.

"Ah, there you are, Alissandra," Aunt Ches greeted me. She raised her brows as a smile spread across her face. "Browsing our library?"

I coughed, not sure how to respond.

"No need to be embarrassed. Surely you don't think urges are indecent. We've been cooped up here for an eternity. Gotta let off pent up passion every now and again, somehow. Surely, you've had urges with a charge or two, wishing you could take a tumble through the clouds with them."

My eyes bulged. Mema would have had a heart attack. I'd be lying if I said I hadn't had more than a few thoughts along these lines about Kovis... No, no, I needed to stop. But my brain wouldn't. It took off, running wild. Memories my charges had had of *notable* encounters flooded my consciousness. I seriously needed to divert my attention. But no, my brain persisted.

But instead of replaying more of *those* kinds of events, it began applying reason to the situation, assembling facts like puzzle pieces: It was only my aunts here. Who would they do...? My brain took off at a sprint, heading where it sensed something juicy: Wait. While I'd never known a male, not in *that* way at least, every one of my dream charges who had, Kovis included, had done so with the opposite sex. There were male stewards here of course, but would they... with them? I shook my head. I didn't want to know.

"Would you like to borrow one?" Aunt Nona asked, chuckling, then held that device up and spun it again.

Borrow what? A book? Or a device? My jaw dropped. What other *devices* had she assembled? "No." It came out too loud and too quick. I tried again, "No, thank you. That's okay." It was much too hot in here.

"You two, stop corrupting the maiden," Aunt Ta objected.

"Surely she's seen—" Ches said.

Ta gave her a pointed look, and Ches chuckled, but fell silent.

I wished for a basin of water to wash my mind. I had no idea my ancient aunts were… Some things were definitely better left unknown. I *had* to change the subject. "I take it you decided how long that babe's life would be?" I asked, as I sat back down on one of the divans.

"We did," Nona said. "I'd reworked an old water clock a moon ago so I put it into service for the wee one, for the agreed upon time."

"How do you decide?"

"Decide? What? Which timekeeping device to use?"

"No, how long a human's life will be?"

"That would be our little secret, now wouldn't it?" She raised a brow.

I hunched. I felt like I'd asked a forbidden question. But wait… I shook my head. They kept this a secret, but not the other? Surely the other should have been more closely guarded, *especially* around my family. Was this why no one ever invited them to family functions, or was it truly my family's respect—fear more like—of their power that kept them at a distance? I'd been led to believe the latter, but I could certainly believe the former. I pinched my bottom lip. No, this was my aunts' battle to fight, not mine. I had enough to deal with, with Father. They could do whatever they wanted so long as they didn't keep me from doing what I wanted. I chortled to myself, like that would ever happen.

"So, where were we? Ah, yes, your charge as a youngster. You shared a couple incidents, but let me ask, did you have any *concerns* about him in his formative years?" Aunt Ta asked as they settled back to listen to more of Kovis's tale.

Did they have a list of questions they were running down? It sounded that way. I hedged, "Can you define formative?"

"Up to eight annums of age."

Crap! I'd hoped they wouldn't ask. The first of many events I'd never forget had started as the twins turned eight. I held my breath as I thought about what story to invent to cover the unpleasantness that filled my mind. But then again, it hadn't been Kovis's fault, perhaps I'd leave my interpretative storytelling for if they asked about more recent events. It seemed a reasonable bet they'd ask.

I exhaled as I began.

"The twins had celebrated their eighth birthday, and while they'd thrilled at each being given a horse as a gift..." My chest constricted. "... that night, Emperor Altairn barged into the nursery yelling 'You killed her!' He slurred his words and waved a nearly empty bottle."

All three of my aunts' heads snapped back.

"Kovis and Kennan had been playing with soldiers on the floor. Nanny Leida motioned the boys behind her and they bolted for her skirts.

"Leida bowed. 'My emperor, what a surprise to see you this evening.' She kept her tone light.

"'That's right, go hide behind a woman's skirts. You killed her.' The emperor shouted, waving and pointing."

I bit my lip.

Ta's eyes grew large. "What brought this on?"

"'She was the love of my life, and you killed her.' That's what he said."

"Was he referring to his late wife?" Nona asked, leaning forward.

"Alfreda and I suspect so. He accused the twins of being murderers just after naming them, so it would make sense."

Nona and Ches shared a look at the revelation.

"Go on," Ches said, rolling her shoulders.

"The nanny pleaded with him, 'Majesty, please. It's late.'"

I huffed.

"His reply? 'Yes, it is too late. And it's all their fault.'

"As you might imagine, both boys were scared out of their wits especially when their father swayed and nearly tipped over as he took a step toward them, then threatened to burn them with his flames."

A chill raced up my back. I could still hear the terror in Leida's voice.

Nona sucked in a breath.

"'Step aside and let me at 'em.' The emperor said, then raised a hand. I honestly thought he'd burn them with his Fire magic."

I swallowed, trying to calm my breathing.

Aunt Ta rubbed the back of her neck.

"He stumbled closer and Leida spread her arms wide, refusing to move."

"Bravo, she's a good woman." Ta brought her head down sharply.

Nona fingered one of her mechanisms. Ches clutched her robe.

I exhaled, remembering what happened next.

"Four guards burst through the nursery door and 'helped' the emperor away."

Aunt Ches and Nona both let out a long breath. Ta shook her head.

"I'm sorry. I didn't want to tell you, but you asked."

Ta waved a hand. "No, you were right to do so. It is part of who your charge has become. Do not apologize for what is not his doing."

"I'd heard the emperor call the twins 'murderers' not long after they'd been born." Ches and Nona gave me long looks. "But it's the first time Kovis heard it. As you might guess, it's impacted him significantly."

Nona's shoulders slumped. Ches's eyes went dull.

My aunts sat contemplating—recovering, more like—for several heartbeats.

Ta had responded reasonably, thank the Ancient One. I couldn't yet judge Nona or Ches.

Yet they'd ended that one human's life in such a calloused manner.

My stomach clenched.

Would they end Kovis's life similarly if I couldn't convince them he was worth saving?

Chapter Twenty-Seven

Ancel stopped not far away and looked at Aunt Ta, before clearing his throat. "You asked me to retrieve you at the time appointed to extinguish the twenty-three-annum female."

"Thank you, that I did," Ta replied.

I sucked in air, not again. My heart sped. She would end another young human life. I couldn't just sit idly by and say nothing. "Do you have to?"

Four sets of eyes met mine but I refused to be intimidated. I didn't know this woman, but it didn't matter. Perhaps I identified with her, seeing her as no different than Kovis. I would take a stand and defend her right to continue living.

Aunt Ches raised an eyebrow. "You presume to know how best to shepherd humans?"

She made it sound like she saw humans as sheep. Sheep were frail and stupid. Is that what she thought of them? I swallowed. "He said she's only twenty-three. She's so young. Surely you could grant her more time?"

"Report," she said to Ancel.

The steward clasped his hands behind his back and said, "The maiden has been sick and dying for quite some time. She married at seventeen, and she and her husband are madly in love. They had a child three annums ago and she's enjoyed watching him grow. She has lived a full and meaningful life despite her illness."

"Oh... I...." I hadn't thought about circumstances such as sickness.

"Would you have us prolong her agony? Prolong her husband and child's pain at seeing her like this, a mere shadow of who she once was?" Aunt Nona said, picking up her yellow sash and running it across her palms.

Ancel continued, "Last eve, her husband pleaded with the Ancient One to take her and end her suffering."

Aunt Nona smiled warmly. "Child, do you honestly believe we would take a human life capriciously?"

"I... Uh..."

Ta rose. "If you'll excuse me." She changed back into her gray robe and shawl, then followed the steward out.

Ches put a hand on my knee. "You mean well... so do we. We take our responsibilities seriously. Humans are relatively fragile, and I try to take all the variables that could impact their lives into account when I set the length for each."

"You said before that sometimes accidents happen to end a human life before the time you allot. Was this one of those times?"

Aunt Ches shook her head. "No, I recall setting the suns this woman would enjoy. I knew."

She knew? How could she possibly know the woman would contract an illness that would kill her?

As if listening to my thoughts, Ches smiled. "You're passionate about humans and making their lives more pleasing. I like that about you. It's an admirable quality. I wish more sand beings were like you."

"We all do," Aunt Nona chimed in.

My aunts were praising me for caring. I didn't know what to say. How could I not? Being a sandmaiden was more than just a craft to me. I shifted my leg, mirroring the movement of my thoughts. I'd been vacillating between trusting them or not. But they'd just shown me they really did care about humans.

My mind tried to fit the pieces together. Kovis's life was at stake. Yet, their care for this sick woman felt genuine and authentic, certainly not staged. And they were showing me a side of themselves I doubted many saw with their wild clothes and especially that library. Call me crazy, but my gut told me I could trust them, and it was rarely wrong—well, except in Father's case.

But what about that first human life they'd snuffed out? It still didn't sit well.

We'd always been told my aunts were fearsome and never to be trifled with. I'd witnessed that with Aunt Ta stopping time for those mares—her actions had underscored everything I'd ever heard. But what they'd shown me about themselves was counter to all that.

Was it possible I'd misinterpreted what had happened? I didn't know the circumstances surrounding that other human's life. What if it was some old human ready to enter Light realm after a hard life? Or perhaps it had been another sick human. What I had believed about my aunts had colored my perspective, and I'd viewed that short exchange the only way I could, as cold and uncaring. But what if it had been anything but...

I exhaled as a sense of reassurance filled me that they would listen to reason and wouldn't judge Kovis harshly regardless of the lies Father had probably told them. I realized that my aunts may be older than time itself, but as a result, they possessed wisdom, and I doubted whether even Father, the most powerful king in Dream, could influence them unduly.

"We've been talking about your concern for humans, so let's get back to your dream charge," Aunt Ches said.

"We sense, how shall we say..." Aunt Nona paused to phrase her words just so. "...a greater darkness in him."

How had they picked up on that? I sighed heavily. I didn't know how they knew, but my game was up. Good thing I'd started to trust them because I wasn't pulling anything over on them. They hadn't been kidding when they'd said honesty was a virtue and not much else would serve me here.

I bit my lip. I had to tell them Kovis's whole story. As with all of the other influences, it had made him who he had become. They needed to know. Still I hesitated.

"Take your time," Ches encouraged.

I nodded, thinking through where to begin. At length I said, "It all began when Kovis was ten."

"He'd noticed Rasa had been quieter than usual and not just for one sun, or two. He couldn't remember exactly when it began, sometime around when his father had returned from the war, but it troubled him. I worked on helping him make sense of it as I wove his dreams, but I'll never forget the night I figured it all out."

I bounced my foot.

"The emperor had just returned from the front for the winter. As he greeted the children, Rasa stepped forward and he spoke quiet words as he stroked her back. Rasa bit her lip when he was done, and Kovis asked her what was wrong, but she just shrugged it off. So Kovis didn't think anything more of it.

"But she started skipping meals which annoyed their father to no end. She told Kovis she was just tired. Well, time went on and their father returned to the front. Next thing I knew, Rasa's powers manifested and Kovis was excited for her *despite* how it happened."

I rolled my eyes.

Aunt Ches furrowed her brow. "What happened?"

"Rasa had just turned thirteen so it stood to reason she'd manifest soon, but those two…" I shook my head.

Nona leaned in.

"Kovis and Kennan had been studying under Master Readingham, the weapons master, learning how to wield swords. Well, they wanted to show off, so they dragged Rasa out to the weapons training yard and proceeded to outline the rules they would abide by as they jousted." I glanced my aunts over. "To really impress their sister, they decided to use real weapons, rather than the wooden training swords they'd used so far."

"Why do I feel like something bad happened?" Ches asked, fingering the sash of her robe.

"Let her speak," Nona said, frowning.

I grinned, building up the nasty story.

"Despite Rasa questioning the wisdom of using sharp, metal weapons, they convinced her they knew what they were doing. Anyway, so they assumed ready positions and Rasa called for them to begin.

"They circled, around and around, both feigning an attack now and then. At length, Kennan made good on his threat and brandished his sword with flair. Kovis blocked. Kennan followed up. Another block. Metal clanged as Kennan struck again. Back and forth. Back and forth. You get the idea. But Master Readingham spotted them at some point."

Nona sighed. "Glad someone finally put a stop to it."

"But nothing bad had happened yet," Ches objected.

"'Princes!'" I tried making my voice deep to mimic the man. "He shouted across the training yard and Kovis looked over. Unfortunately..."

"Oh, no." Nona bit her nails.

Ches scrunched her face.

"Kennan was mid-stroke and he brought his blade down on Kovis's ear."

Nona yipped.

Ches's eyes grew wide.

"Rasa screamed, right along with Kovis, as well as Kennan, who held himself, clearly horrified at what he'd done. Blood seeped between Kovis's fingers and started running down his cheek. Oh, it was awful. Kovis was in so much pain. You can imagine."

My aunts sat frozen.

"Master Readingham and a host of trainees converged and he started yelling orders to stay back, to give Kovis room, to grab rags to staunch the bleeding, and the like, all while Kovis writhed on the ground."

Nona clenched her teeth and shook her head.

"Rasa ignored the man and knelt beside Kovis. She told him she felt strange, but a 'good' strange, whatever that meant, and she told Kovis to move his hands aside. Kovis gave her a long look, but finally did and blood gushed from the wound."

"Oh, no," Ches moaned, biting her lip.

"Rasa's hands trembled as she closed her eyes and moved them above his ear. Despite all the soldiers looking on, you could have heard straw fall, it was so quiet. But just heartbeats later, Kovis stopped moaning and relaxed. She'd healed him. Concern for Kovis unleashed had her powers."

Nona and Ches exhaled, loudly.

"Impressive," Ta said. "I trust the princes stuck to wooden practice swords after that?"

Ta was back. I hadn't heard her come in, but I smiled broadly. "Yes. And Kovis still brags that he made her powers manifest."

Nona snickered.

"But back to your charge," Ta said.

Right… They weren't going to be sidetracked.

"Kovis was happy for his sister. She received a healer's apprenticeship as a result. But it meant she moved to an apprentice's room in the healers building and he couldn't see her every sun. He missed her. And that's when…" I shook my head and my stomach twisted.

Ta furrowed her brow. Nona and Ches exchanged glances.

"The emperor was again back from the front and Kovis went looking for him one evening. Their father had begun tutoring Rasa regarding how to rule, so he wasn't surprised when a guard told him that his father and Rasa were working in the conservatory again and had left instructions not to be disturbed. Well, Kovis refused to take 'no' for an answer, so when the guard wasn't looking, he snuck past."

"The conservatory is all glass walls and juts out from the palace. Kovis didn't want to interrupt if his father and Rasa looked like they were deep in conversation, so he paused at a hall window and peered into the nearest clear wall of the room."

"Kovis cocked his head and squinted, unsure what he saw, then moved to a closer window to get a better view. Father and Rasa were talking on the couch and he looked happy, his smile said so, as he stroked Rasa's back. He comforted her for some reason."

I scanned my aunts. There'd be no going back once I told them what happened next.

"Go on, child," Ta encouraged.

I rubbed my hands and nodded.

"Rasa's eyes grew large as she and her father moved to the chaise and she lay down. Kovis could only see his father's back and was surprised when he knelt at Rasa's feet. He'd never seen his father do that before. He wondered if their father was going to give Rasa a foot massage to help her feel better. But the man reached for the hem of Rasa's green apprentice robe and slowly pushed it up."

Ches sucked in a breath. Nona drew a hand to her mouth. Ta clasped her hands together.

"His father pulled Rasa by her thighs to the end of the chaise and spread her legs apart. Rasa clutched the side of the divan and looked away."

"No," Aunt Ta said, shaking her head.

My heart raced, the same as the first time I'd seen it.

"Kovis didn't understand what he was seeing, but even at eleven, he knew it was wrong. And then his father moved his hips forward. Kovis didn't wait. He burst through the conservatory door yelling for his father to stop."

"Good boy," Nona said, raising a fist.

"Well, as you might expect, the man didn't agree. Kovis froze at the sight of his father's bare manhood standing tall a hairsbreadth from Rasa's... parts. Rasa struggled to close her legs, but she couldn't, not with his father kneeling there. She fumbled to sit up and pull her robe down, but her father held her down."

"Animal!" Nona shouted.

"Kovis rushed his father, begging him to let Rasa go, but he was wiry and couldn't push the man away. His father cursed him, then grabbed his shirt collar with both hands."

Ches straightened. Nona held her breath. Ta's eyes grew large.

"'Rasa, run!' Kovis screamed it as he fought his father's grip. Rasa scrambled off the chaise and bolted from the room, but the emperor wasn't done with Kovis."

"Ancient One, have mercy." Ta drew a hand to her throat.

"His father punched Kovis in the gut. He doubled over and fell to the floor, unable to breathe."

My heart ached.

Ches shook her head.

"After the man put himself together, he swore that if Kovis breathed a word of what he'd seen to anyone, he'd hurt him worse."

Ta closed her eyes.

"The abuse was bad enough, but what was worse, Kovis blamed himself. Rasa had always protected him and Kennan, but he hadn't been there to protect her when she most needed him."

"That poor boy." Nona held her stomach.

Ches swiped at the corner of an eye, and that's all it took for the tears that had welled up in me, to fall.

Ta sighed.

My voice quivered as I continued. "I tried to convince him it wasn't his fault as I wove his dreams. The signs had been subtle and he'd never been exposed to anything so horrific, so he wouldn't know to look. But he refused to be comforted."

"Oh, child," Nona said.

My aunts enveloped me in a hug.

At length, I recomposed myself and pulled back. "You're... you're not going to..."

I glanced between them, searching their eyes, but they'd collected themselves as well and I couldn't read them.

My heart sped. I'd said too much. "He's strong. He'll recover... please..."

"Calm yourself, child." Ta leaned back.

My breathing labored. What did that mean?

Chapter Twenty-Eight

"Yes, Corwin." Aunt Nona turned her attention from my hyperventilating and acknowledged another steward who stood holding three books.

"These just arrived from Argatha."

I bit my lip. Not more of *those* books.

"Very good, hand them here." Nona placed them on her lap. I caught the titles: *Hot and Wild Ride, Blazing Saddles,* and *Naughty but Nice.*

I tried to hide my discomfort, drawing my arms about myself.

Turning to me, Aunt Ta said, "Your charge has been through a lot with his sister." Her voice was soft. "He's seen his share of trials, no doubt about it. Has it affected his intimacy with women?"

"What... What do you mean?" Is *that* all they ever thought about? I'd just poured out my heart and she was asking about his intimacy?

I shifted. Or perhaps it meant I hadn't ruined everything. They wouldn't care to know more if they were going to end him, would they?

Nona placed a hand on my leg. "That was a horrible experience to be sure, but don't take offense at her question. She means no disrespect."

I nodded. "I'm sorry. Can you repeat your question?"

Aunt Ta clarified. "Let me rephrase. Has your charge put the emperor's actions into proper perspective?"

Nona added. "You've shaped his thoughts as you've woven his dreams. Is he healthy in how he views the fairer sex or have events completely…"

"Warped his view?" I finished for her.

"Well put. Yes, perverted his view," Nona said. "Does he view women as things to be used?"

Their clarification brought understanding and calmed me. "No, he doesn't."

Aunt Ta leaned back. "Few things reveal a person's perspective more clearly than sex where everything is laid bare, in more ways than one. So tell us then, how *has* he developed sexually?"

I hated the question. They believed sex revealed a being's innermost perspective on, not just… the physical act, but life as a whole. I'd *never* made that leap before. It *was* all they thought about.

I cleared my throat. But as I did, I realized that trauma hadn't caused my aunts to decide to end him prematurely. At least it didn't seem so. What *would* tip those scales?

I exhaled and refocused, but as I mulled their question it felt as if I would be revealing the most intimate and private part of Kovis's life. I would be. I shook my head. But if I couldn't show that Kovis hadn't been warped by his horrific experiences… would they end him? Oh Dyeus, no. I could hold nothing back. Privacy and modesty weren't important enough to put him in jeopardy.

I told them the tale of Kovis's first intimate encounter with a female when he was fifteen, during the Lightning Ball.

My aunts smiled and grinned, as well as cursed the emperor throughout my telling. And rightfully so.

But when I reached the end, Aunt Ches said, "So it seems he was aware of how perverted his father was and he was seeking to understand what healthy love is."

"Yes, he's seen how disgusting and damaging…"

"It's okay, call it what it is… incest," Aunt Ta agreed.

I nodded. "He hasn't had a role model, and he knows it. He's had to figure it out on his own."

"Good for him for being aware of it and seeking to understand what's healthy. I applaud him," Aunt Nona said as she made the device sing once more.

She'd praised Kovis. I drew a hand to my heart. That had to be a positive for him, no?

"You said he was fifteen and curious. He's twenty-five now. What is he like in terms of his current view of women?" Aunt Ta probed.

My heart climbed into my throat. I'd have to tell them about Dierna—I only barely suppressed a growl—and how the wench had crushed him. Despite the pain, I didn't think it had changed his view of women, much less life, at least his nighttime thoughts hadn't revealed that. But would my aunts agree?

I sighed as I began. "As you would know, the emperor died when Kovis was twenty-one. Rasa was finally safe, but he didn't know how to work through the trauma of the abuse he and his siblings had endured. He was introduced to Lady Dierna, a wealthy lesser Lord's daughter from Metal province, at the spring equinox ball not long after and he took an immediate liking to her wavy locks and bubbly personality.

"Understandably, Kovis started out the relationship cautiously, always taking care to treat her with respect and dignity. He took her to the theater, walking, and riding. They talked for hours, and he found he could tell her anything and everything. She listened and never judged him, no matter how dark the story he related. She made him feel emotionally safe, and he poured out his heart to her. I can't tell you how happy I was for him."

But my smile faded.

"Kovis had brought her to his bed and they enjoyed making love. At least it seemed it was love."

Ches shifted.

"Well one sun, Kovis's work finished early and he decided to surprise Dierna. Male that he was, he thought they might 'enjoy' each other a bit."

I stifled a smile, knowing what came next.

"He reached his rooms and noticed Ricker, his guard who should have been on duty, wasn't outside his door like usual."

Ches drew a hand over her mouth.

"The man was a handpicked member of his personal security detail, so he thought nothing of it. He assumed he'd find him inside checking on one thing or another. So he opened the door quietly. Surveying the common area, he didn't spot Dierna so he crept forward on light feet, excitement gathering in his gut with each step."

Nona bit a finger of her fisted hand.

"A moan reached him as he neared the bedroom. He abandoned stealth and rushed forward, hands out, ready to unleash the magic of his winds on anyone who dared harm her."

Ta bowed her head, anticipating.

"Kovis burst through the double doors and his world shattered. His trusted guard was in bed with his beloved."

"No!" Nona and Ches exclaimed in unison.

"Guards hauled the traitors out of his rooms, but when the door clicked shut, Kovis stumbled back into the common area, collapsing on the divan before the unlit fireplace. Head in his hands, elbows on knees, his frame shook with the rush of sorrow and pain."

I swiped at the stray tears that found their way down my cheeks. Dierna's betrayal, on top of all that had happened to Rasa, had caused Kovis to shut down emotionally and build a protective wall around his heart. I didn't blame him, but the problem with those kinds of walls is that while they protect from emotional pain, they also forbid feelings, even good ones. His heart had turned to stone, and even though I continued to work on it as I wove his dreams each night, I hadn't made much, if any progress at restoring warmth.

"It would seem, despite the trials, he does still honor women," Aunt Ta said, infusing it with softness as she patted my arm.

Her voice barely more than a whisper, Aunt Ches shifted the conversation, "You care deeply for him, don't you? More than any charge you've had."

I closed my eyes and calmed my breathing. Nona rubbed my shoulder. "I do. He's always been different from the others what with his thrumming powers and being an identical twin, but what made him special was that…" I exhaled heavily. "… he never knew a mother's love and always longed for a close a close relationship with his father." I paused. Debating. Could I let them see the real me, insecurities and all? I cleared my throat. "Just like me."

All three of my aunts looked at me. Ta was the first to react, closing her eyes and nodding.

I told them about Kovis's longsuffering efforts to win his father's… attention. Yes, attention. He'd certainly never earned the man's affection. I earned more nods.

My heart panged. I hadn't succeeded either. "So I guess you could say—"

"You share the same inner longings," Ches said.

"You've found someone who you feel understands you completely. Who you feel… connected with." Nona drew a hand to her heart.

I bobbed my head. "Kovis is a *very* good looking man, especially now that he's filled out." I grinned, thinking of his muscled chest. "His thrum makes him… very seductive. And his beautiful eyes… don't get me started." Nona chuckled. But a heartbeat later, I let my smile fade as I returned from my tangent. "But that connection… that's what makes him different than the others. Sand people don't fall in love with their charges, but I think I may have."

I leaned back and my aunts again exchanged looks. They didn't smile, only starred into each other's eyes, somehow communicating.

What were they saying amongst themselves?

I'd been vulnerable. They'd told me our conversation was as much about me as it was Kovis. Well, I'd held nothing back. I hadn't planned to, but it had all poured out. And now they judged me, judged us.

My breathing hitched and I bit my lip as the silence dragged on.

Chapter Twenty-Nine

Shouts echoed through the swirling door.

I'd never seen Ancel or Corwin dramatic much less emotional, but their eyes were wide as they came to an abrupt stop near where we sat. "We have company."

"Who is it?" Aunt Ta asked.

The stewards looked me up and down. I shifted. Why were they staring at me? And what had my aunts concluded?

Ta chuckled and said, "Alissandra, it appears your rescuers have arrived. I wondered how long it would take them to track you down."

"My rescuers?"

"Unless I miss my guess, none other than the god of sleep and his beautiful bride, Pasithea." Nona smiled.

Grandfather and Mema? How did she know? But they'd come? How had they found me?

My aunts rose and shed their colorful robes then replaced them with the drab gray of earlier, such a shame. The sharp contrast brought forth how different they were from their public personas.

The red-velvet of Aunt Ta's under-dress disappeared as Corwin helped arrange the gray robe around her wings in back. "We ask you not to divulge what you have seen and experienced with us."

I nodded. "But what did you decide about my charge?" My heart raced.

Ta turned, and without emotion, asked, "What do you think we decided?"

I opened and closed my mouth as my stomach went hard. "I... I don't know. I'm hoping you chose to leave him be."

Aunt Ta turned and headed for the swirling door.

My breathing labored.

"Not what you expected, are we?" Aunt Ches asked.

"You're definitely different than I ever imagined. I had this picture of you like old crones, serious and stiff." I forced a smile. They hadn't answered my question.

"We are who we need to be for a specific audience," Aunt Ches replied, ignoring my angst. "For your father we were as you've been made to believe. You, on the other hand, needed our softer sides to make you comfortable so we could get a reasonable understanding of you and your charge."

I nodded. A reasonable understanding. Is that what they'd gotten? And I still didn't know the outcome.

"Not a word to anyone," Aunt Nona held up a finger.

"I promise." I bit my lip.

Aunts Ches and Nona schooled their expressions as we followed Ta back through the swirling door. The stench of Mare-Rankin and his scruffy ruffians immediately hit us. Their stink had overwhelmed the place in our absence, and my full stomach threatened revolt.

My aunts mounted the dais. I took my time walking toward the mare-leader and his pack of mongrels, breathing through my mouth.

"This way." One of the attendants who guarded the doors to the Hall of Time directed from between towering shelves.

Grandfather and Mema strode forward with all twenty-one of my siblings and our guards on their heels. My siblings' steps shuddered and several gasps escaped them when they spotted Mare-Rankin and his minions, but they continued forward.

My brothers all looked pissed along with Velma and Wynnfrith. Eolande, Amelia, and Farfelee bit a lip or rubbed an arm. The rest frowned, stole sidelong glances, and covered their noses. Clearly, Mema was worried, for while she hid it well, the fact that she didn't correct any of their unmaidenly behavior, betrayed her anxiety.

"Ali," Alfreda called. "Thank the Ancient One you're okay." Mema again didn't react.

"Move aside," Aunt Ta commanded Mare-Rankin. "Your fetid fiends, too."

My family stopped before the dais and bowed low.

"Rise," Aunt Ta said.

Grandfather shook his head. "Sisters, I'm surprised at you, forcing Alissandra before you."

"That wasn't our doing," Aunt Ches replied.

"Your son accomplished that," Aunt Nona added.

"Well, you haven't granted her the opportunity to leave that I can see. So I'll hold you equally responsible."

Nona and Ches shrugged, and Ta explained, "A request was put to us. We cared not the way the respondent arrived, only that she did."

"Well, unless you want me making a mess of things..." He glanced about the hall. "I suggest you release Alissandra to me."

"You would threaten us?" Ta sat up straight and drew a hand to her chest.

Grandfather raised a brow. "You have much to lose."

I drew in a breath. This wasn't going well.

Mema put a hand on Grandfather's arm. "Alissandra is our granddaughter. Surely you can't fault us for protecting her."

"Very well. We have what we needed from her anyway," Ta said.

"And that is?" Grandfather asked.

"Father wanted them to eliminate Kovis," I charged.

Murmuring erupted from my siblings. If Father could pull a stunt like this with my dream charge, he could do it to any one of theirs as well.

"Is this true?" Grandfather's voice grew cold.

"We never said that."

"What? Yes..." I grabbed a lock of hair and twisted. Had I misunderstood? How was that possible? "Then what?"

"That, Alissandra, is a confidential matter. Let's just say we see your protectiveness and heart for your charge. If he were a horrible human, you would feel differently about him."

"And?"

"We have everything we need to make a determination concerning the request your father made," Ta said.

"What are you going to do?" My pitch rose. After everything I'd... Had they been playing me, no different from Father?

"You will know soon enough," Ches said.

I took to bouncing. I'd hoped, prayed they'd decide in Kovis's favor, was I wrong? And Father hadn't wanted Kovis eliminated? Then what? What could he possibly have asked for?

"Think, Alissandra." Nona locked eyes with me.

What was I supposed to think? What were they going to do to Kovis?

Ches and Ta joined their staring contest, and the weight of their stares made me settle. They couldn't be who I'd discovered them to be, not in public. They knew how I felt about Kovis and understood his story.

As if reading my thoughts, Aunt Ta nodded.

I inhaled sharply. Was she really saying what I hoped? I held Ta's gaze, afraid if I let it drop, I'd realize I'd let sunshine and rainbows triumph once more. Did she really mean what I prayed she did?

Ches and Nona added nods of their own.

I exhaled as my heart soared, but a stern look from Ta stifled a grin. I mimicked their nods instead.

Velma and Alfreda wrinkled their brows. They'd surely be asking questions.

Ta glanced around the room. Several tan-robed attendants held their noses, others looked pale. She turned her attention to the mares who hadn't taken their gazes from her and her sisters. "You've accomplished your task, but stunk up our fine hall. Kindly remove yourselves at once. You're making my stewards ill."

Several mares snarled. Mare-Rankin hushed them.

I swallowed. Several of my siblings' eyes grew large.

"If my attendants can't perform their duties... the Ancient One himself will be, not a little upset with you, orders or no. So unless you're prepared to, shall we say, pay for the problems you create by *servicing* the gods he specifies, in whatever form they desire you take..." More snarls erupted from the wolfish beasts. "I suggest you hide your tails between your legs, slink out of here, and go back to the caves you crawled out of."

Aunt Ta pushed back her shoulders. Ches leaned back and steepled her fingers. Nona smirked and flexed her wings.

I couldn't help but snicker to myself. My siblings seemed inclined to do the same. These monsters deserved everything they were getting at my aunts' hands. We had no influence over mares, trained or wild, and our charges always bore the brunt. Were my aunts exacting some sort of vengeance on them, for us, because they could? I chose to believe so.

Mare-Rankin made no reply but motioned his troops to form up and follow him. They'd taken no more than two steps when Aunt Ta stopped them. "I believe I said to hide your tails between your legs and slink out of here. You, too." She nodded at Mare-Rankin.

Rankin gave an incredulous stare, but shifted into his base wolfish form. Phina and Ailith shrieked at the sight but my wonderful brother, the real Rankin, crossed his arms and assumed a commanding stance. Several others of my brothers did the same and smiles abounded among my family.

"Now slink!" Aunt Ta commanded. Her furled wings stood taller.

The mare leader gave a bark and howl, and he, plus all twenty-one mares, plus their three fake guards drew their tails between their legs. Ears flattened and growls erupted, but they ever so slowly, step after deliberate step, made their way out of the Hall of Time.

The doors thudded shut, and I could tell my family wanted to engulf me in hugs, but the imposing presence my aunts created held them in check.

"Open the windows, let's get some fresh air in here," Aunt Ches declared.

Grandfather took charge and said, "Sisters, thank you for that. It was pleasantly unexpected. We wish not to bother you further so now that we've found who we came for, with your permission, we'll take our leave."

"Not so quick," Aunt Ches objected.

My siblings sucked in a breath and the sound of wings ruffling rose.

"With favors, come favors." Ta raised a brow.

"What would you have us do in return?" Mema asked before Grandfather could let loose something he would regret.

My three aunts shared looks, then nods, and Aunt Nona said, "We need new reading material, a very specific type of reading material. Alissandra knows what will satisfy us."

Everyone turned and looked at me. I tried to cover my warming cheeks as I brought my hands up.

"Once every moon, she will deliver new books to us."

Grandfather cocked his head. "And we're to believe you'll let her leave after delivering this 'reading material' to you?"

"Of course, how could she deliver more the next moon if we detained her?"

"May we have a heartbeat?" Mema asked.

My aunts nodded.

Grandfather and Mema bowed their heads together and consulted in whispers. Hand gestures, wing ruffling, and a myriad of facial expressions on both their parts, later and Grandfather finally stood back and said, "It is agreed."

I stifled a grin. They'd gotten me to bring them more naughty books. Perhaps it was their way of beginning a dialogue with my family that hadn't existed. If so, it was a *huge* gap they were attempting to bridge.

But they wouldn't harm Kovis, the thought again sent a thrill through me. But on its heels, my stomach soured. Father would soon know, too.

He never took well to losing.

Chapter Thirty

I raised a brow when Grandfather bowed. Even the god of sleep bowed to my aunts? But we all followed his example.

Aunt Ta finally allowed us to rise.

I joined my grandparents and received engulfing hugs from both. But before we got carried away, Grandfather said, "I believe we should adjourn before we trouble your great aunts further."

No one uttered a word as we turned, I between Mema and Grandfather at the head of the group. Mema extended a wing and pulled me close.

I glanced back at my aunts. They sat stone-faced, watching our procession, revealing nothing of what they might be thinking, holding their public façade without fail. Aunt Ta caught the gesture of a steward not far from us and nodded. Several of my siblings watched the brown-robed assistant snuff out a candle.

"Did she just..." Bega's pitch rose. Several of my other sisters yelped behind me. Despite understanding how much my aunts cared for humans, it still hit me. My aunts had power over life itself, and while they seemed to have accustomed themselves with their role, I doubted I would ever get used to watching that happen.

A collective exhale sounded the heartbeat the doors to the Hall of Time closed behind us, but Grandfather held up a hand to stay our celebrations. "Outside first," he warned.

We wound our way back down the mountain of stairs and finally reached the main foyer. Heading out that ancient front door, there wasn't a mare in sight, good. No doubt they'd beaten a path back to Father's palace to tell all.

One of our guards had barely secured the door when Cuthbert, Deor, and Harding grabbed me and spun me around, swallowing me in a collective embrace. Squealing and laughter and all manner of raucous celebrations rose. I was free and back in the arms of my loving family.

When some of the noise died down, Clovis joked, "Perhaps I'll arrange my hair into the shape of a mare with its tail tucked between its legs." Even Mema laughed at that.

And then the questions began. "Are you okay? What happened? How did they kidnap you?" These and more spilled from my siblings. I told them how the mares had disguised themselves to look like them, how they'd tricked me, covering their noxious stench with an even stronger perfume, how I'd grown suspicious when they didn't act like their normal selves out of the public eye—that produced a number of jokes—and more.

"How did you realize I was gone and how did you find me?" I asked when I finished.

Deor stepped forward and said, "When you didn't meet us in the atrium like we'd told everyone to, we weren't surprised." She winked. I forced a frown and chuckles rippled. "Anyway, Wynnfrith went and checked your room to find you weren't there. We'd noticed that perfume smell while we searched high and low for you. Grandfather and Mema who had been trying to keep Father occupied while we departed, realized he'd acted much too amicably after that dinner rant. They confronted him and he told us what he'd done."

"Good thing, too, or I don't know if we'd have ever found you," Rankin said.

"I think he figured there was no way we'd ever try to rescue you, not with *their* reputations, but oh how wrong he was," Velma said. Several heads bobbed.

With the barrage of questions answered, my siblings changed the conversation to other, lighter topics. Happy chatter replaced scared silence. Mema kept smiling at Grandfather and he kept winking at her.

"Enough seriousness. It's time to celebrate. We found you and you're safe," Grandfather said. "I think we should go to the mushroom caves. It's where you were headed to begin."

Cheers erupted but Mema frowned. "It's getting late. All their charges need their dreams woven."

"Oh, dear, how often can we celebrate something like this?"

"Not often, I should hope!"

We all laughed at that. We were all tired—not one of us had slept in way too long, but none of us would decline a chance to go to the mushroom caves.

"They can weave dreams there. Come on, let's have some fun. Alissandra deserves it," Grandfather said. Then in a whisper that I overheard, he added, "Maybe you and I can do a little something while they're occupied?"

Mema's cheeks pinked and I knew we wouldn't be headed home anytime soon. We launched into the air without another challenge. The sounds of chatter and beating wings filled the air. It felt so good to be surrounded by love.

The sun was casting our shadows long across the landscape as we flew north. The top of my shadow head as well as those of the rest of my family skimmed the calm waters of the sea off to our right.

We'd flown some distance when Velma moved beside me in formation. I couldn't forget what she'd revealed earlier this morning about being used by Father to accomplish his ends. She didn't say anything for quite a while, but her periodic looks spoke volumes. My gut told me she was thinking about what Father might do next.

Me, too.

But I wasn't prepared when she asked, "What did Aunt Ta mean when she said you know the kinds of books they like?"

My brows shot up and my cheeks warmed. Little traitors. "Oh, um—"

Velma tilted her head. She never let things that raised her suspicions, go. How far would she probe? I was such a bad liar.

My aunts had made me promise not to divulge anything I'd experienced. And you didn't betray them. If I screwed up and they found out... A rock filled the pit of my stomach.

Chapter Thirty-One

How blitzed would we get? I preferred to wonder about that, rather than worry about Velma's penetrating stare.

I focused on the beautiful sunset as we touched down on the sandy beach—the fiery red sphere had turned the clouds a brilliant orange.

Velma kept eyeing me, although no one said a word as we watched it continue its path, touching, then hugging the hills of Lemnos.

I tried to let the waves lapping the shore calm me. I tried. Half, then a quarter, then finally just a sliver of the sun shown until the ball of fire bid us goodnight, and left a pink sky as a promise of its return.

I attempted to push my angst aside as we traipsed over to the face of the sheer, white cliff and ducked as we passed single file into the passage. Green iridescent fungus on water-slicked rock walls illuminated the path, and a distinctive damp, musty smell soon filled my nose. I heard water dripping ahead, and I started singing a lullaby.

Lavender's blue, dilly dilly, lavender's green,
When I am king, dilly dilly, you shall be queen:
Who told you so, dilly dilly, who told you so?
'Twas mine own heart, dilly dilly, that told me so.

My siblings picked up the tune, and we were all singing or humming as we reached the open area in which mushrooms grew taller than any of us. We affectionately called it the mushroom forest, although to call it that didn't really make sense considering it grew inside the rocks and one could not see the sky.

But like a forest, it had several layers—small baby mushrooms that your foot could easily topple, medium mushrooms that came to your knees, others, some skinny, some stocky, that stretched all the way to your shoulders, and still others that were taller and broader yet. We tried to avoid the water filled dips that populated the path to only modest success and my feet were soon soaked, but it didn't dampen my singing.

Call up your men, dilly dilly, set them to work,
Some with a rake, dilly dilly, some with a fork;
Some to make hay, dilly dilly, some to thresh corn,
Whilst you and I, dilly dilly, keep ourselves warm.

Grandfather belted out the last verse from behind us as I picked one of the brightly glowing baby 'shrooms—the youngest were always the brightest. I sniffed it, then popped it into my mouth. *Mmm.* Most mushrooms were bland, but the ones here always tasted sweet to me. Perhaps it was whatever made them glow, doing it. No matter, I knew my angst would soon be gone and I'd be feeling... really good. My siblings were foraging, too. We knew what we were doing. Good thing Kovis wouldn't need me right away. This was to be a celebration and it definitely would be at this rate. I sung all the louder.

If you should die, dilly dilly, as it may hap,

• • •

You shall be buried, dilly dilly, under the tap;
Who told you so, dilly dilly, pray tell me why?
That you might drink, dilly dilly, when you are dry.

Lullabies were created by both humans and sand people alike. This song had to have been created by a human somewhere in Wake realm because it made no sense to me, but no one cared. I loved the tune all the same. My not caring increased exponentially as we turned right and I caught the bluish glow we sought. We had arrived.

Good size blue crystals sprouted from the cavern, illuminating the shallow water that created the damp environment that was so perfect for these plants. These were a shorter variety than the ones we'd passed through. It seemed these required much more water. And they got it judging by the clumps of mushrooms growing everywhere—from the walls, the ceiling, as well as the floor.

I sat on the edge of the shallows and took my boots off. Several of my siblings joined me, rolling up our pants and dipping our feet in the warm water. We'd all eaten several more mushrooms, and everyone was loosening up, at least judging by the boisterous laughter from a brother or two. I was feeling… happy. Yes, really, really happy, and I told my little sister Farfelee, "This is… gre…ate." I hiccupped.

She giggled, clearly enjoying the airy, blissful, unattached sensation as much as me.

My toes had shriveled by the time I pulled them out. The tip of one of my wings dislodged two mushrooms as I grabbed my boots and tried to stand and steady myself. "Oops…" I slurred the s and giggled because I sounded like a snake.

I stumbled but caught myself as I retreated to my favorite alcove. Most of my brothers spread out around the space, then stretched out, leaning against a boulder, a crystal, or just sprawling across the floor, arms behind their head. Grandfather and Mema thought they'd snuck off, but as soon as they disappeared around a bend, my sisters and I followed suit in maximizing our comfort, unmaidenly or not. It had been a long time since I'd felt so free, and I allowed myself to bask, unconstrained and uninhibited.

Despite the number of us, once everyone settled, no one spoke or made any other sound. Rather, we all listened to the plunk, plunk, drip, drip, and gurgling of the water and allowed our thoughts to take us where they willed.

I don't know how long I stayed that way but much of the blissful mushroom mind fog had dissipated and I reached out to Kovis, knowing his presence would make this experience even more perfect. I pictured the dream canopy in my mind, then joining it. I imagined thrusting my wings out wide and soaring on calm air, down, down, down to the palace in Veritas.

I found Kovis's thought thread easily enough, a relief based on what I'd woven last night. Kovis's thread again waved erratically as if trying to attract my attention, making sure I couldn't miss it. I told myself this behavior was because he valued me as the primary source of the answers I offered to his challenges.

He'd retired recently, and I threw a handful of dream sand onto his thread. Heartbeats later, he slumbered and his thoughts flowed fast and furious. Good thing much of the mushroom effect had worn off, I would again have my hands full.

Kovis had celebrated his twenty-fifth birthday with his twin last sun and his thoughts about the celebration had caused me a lot of work—what should have been a happy, festive occasion, proved anything but for my prince. He'd endured so much pain in his life, and he couldn't find light in his darkness. The depth of his despair had particularly troubled me. I'd had to carefully weave the few strands of hope I'd found, through his melancholy. I feared he might harm himself if I wasn't thorough.

I watched as his memories of this sun replayed, trying to assess the situation before modifying anything.

"Good morning, my prince. Would you like me to saddle Alshain for you?" a groom asked as Kovis strode into the stables.

"No need, Louvel. I'll do it myself."

The sun had only recently risen, and as he headed down a long row of box stalls, most of the equines were busy at their feed boxes. Only their twitching ears peeked over the wall. He stopped at a half door above which a royal blue sign with the insignia of a swooping altairn, talons extended, declared, "Alshain, mount of Crown Prince Kovis Altairn."

Kovis deposited a handful of white primroses on the ledge just outside the door, then entered and patted the horse's neck. He received a nicker in return. "It's good to see you too, boy. Ready to go for a ride?" Alshain, the tall, charcoal destrier, bobbed his head and Kovis set to work.

White primroses in hand, Kovis rode his stallion under the portcullis, out of the gatehouse, and followed the path to the left. The day was gray and overcast, and he knew precipitation would no doubt dampen this sun, fitting as it mirrored his mood. At the fork, he directed Alshain right, up a steep hill, his personal guards following a respectful, yet protective, distance behind.

Alshain trotted up and around a handful of switchbacks, seemingly eager to embrace the freedom despite the gloom. Sensing the horse's eagerness, Kovis increased their pace, letting his stallion run. And he did, hard up the steep hill that overlooked the capital. The crisp air made a chill run up Kovis's back under his royal blue overcoat, but he ignored it, intent on his destination.

Kovis slowed Alshain once they reached the crest of the hill and soon stopped him at the rock wall surrounding the royal burial grounds. He dismounted and secured him to a post.

The hinges of the rusted metal gate protested as Kovis let himself in then surveyed the trove of his forebears. This is where everyone in the royal family ended up, dead and forgotten, no matter what they'd been like in life—Father a case in point. If it weren't for paying stewards to keep the

• • •

weeds at bay and the monuments fit, decay would have her
way.

Hearing his thoughts, I knew the mood I would be dealing with tonight and I braced.

Kovis headed down a row to his left as he did every annum around his birthday. But his mood had never been this "off." He approached a copse of trees, barren of leaves at this point in the annum, and stopped before a thick, smooth stone slab with the emblem of the empire and ornate engraving atop— Emperor Virtus Altairn and his beloved, Empress Onora Altairn. The stone lid rose nearly to his knees.

Kovis's jaw clenched unbidden at seeing his father treated as kindly as his mother. His thoughts swirled. He didn't deserve her. She was too good for him.

I knew Kovis believed this at the very core of his being. Every occasion he'd come to visit his mother since his father's passing four annums before, had added to this sense of injustice.

He placed his handful of white primrose above where he knew his mother lay and sat down on the edge, as if it was the bed of someone sick. The cold of the stone soon bit his legs, adding to his malaise.

"Well, Mother, I turned twenty-five last sun. I know it is hard to believe another annum has come and gone. Kennan and Rasa are doing well. Rasa's becoming a fine empress. She loves the people, it's clear. It's a big challenge ruling the expanded empire. Despite all the improvements and advances we've given them, some of the nonmagical provinces still don't accept that we are all part of one empire.

"We've had rebel attacks that we just can't identify the perpetrators of, but we believe they're insorcel inspired. It's

185

frustrating. But don't you worry; Kennan and I will get to the bottom of things.

"Oh, and Rasa's gotten it in her mind to eliminate some of the brutal practices Father established to keep the new provinces in check. No, she hasn't made it public. She said she never supported the practices, and now that she can do something about it, she plans to. I know, I know. She has a gentle heart and means well. I think she gets it from you, Mother, with that healer's heart you both have. I'm just not sure what might happen if she succeeds. But again, don't you worry. Kennan and I will make her see reason.

"Oh, Kennan? Yes, he's doing fine in his role as Commander of the Guard and Inquest. Most of his duties fit him since he's always been curious. He's solved some really tough cases. He just dislikes interrogating prisoners, but you always have to take the bad with the good, I suppose.

"Me?" Kovis paused, seemingly formulating his thoughts carefully. "Honestly, Mother, I look at life and see how unfair it is, and I wonder what the point is. As far as I can see, no one ever really thrives, you just cope the best you can and then you die, no different than the animals, and I have to ask, is that what I want? Just to cope and then die? What's the point?

Kovis offered a weak chuckle. "I knew you'd ask me that— what do I want to become as a man that would make you proud. You always ask. I'll always support Rasa. I'll make sure she thrives against that conniving council, but I'll just be coping. That can't be all my life is to become, it can't be. There must be more."

Kovis sat for a long time listening to the breeze as well as the chatter of small ground animals as they scurried about their lives, doing what they were meant to do. He noticed and inhaled the scent of the trees, brush, and other plants that the cold weather hadn't scared into hiding, also being and doing exactly what they were meant to be and do.

He stood and meandered over to one of the jumperberry bushes that filled the gaps between the trees of the copse and pulled off a handful of its bright red fruit. Popping it into his mouth, the bitter taste paired well with his thoughts that continued churning.

The world was indifferent to everyone. No one was special. With my other dream charges, while the topic of meaning tended to push them toward despair, that's all it was. I eventually worked them through it, and on they went with their lives. But Kovis was different. I feared his adding an existential crisis concerning meaning might push him over the edge of the abyss of not just despair, but of destruction.

He'd been frozen and emotionally shut down for some time, the unfeelingness a monster all its own. He'd caved to the circumstances life had dealt him and become emotionally withdrawn. I wouldn't let him be satisfied with his current emotional state. It scared him to think about, but he needed to feel again. And until he could feel, worrying about the "meaning of life" would have no purpose. I'd been working on his frozenness on and off for quite some time, but this new darkness renewed my determination to affect change in him.

But first things first, I needed to get Kovis away from the black edge of despair. Kovis had imagined his mother asking him, *what do you want to become as a man that would make me proud of you?* I moved my hands drawing swirls and lines, creating a web of connections, moving images and words around. I modified the imagined question to be, *what would make you proud of yourself, my son?* Kovis moaned in his sleep as the altered thought took root.

Over the course of the night, I added explicit suggestions regarding thawing the frozen condition of his heart. It was an opening, and I'd do everything I could to exploit it for his good.

With the events of the previous sun and now this, I flagged partway through the night. I pinched myself to stay awake.

But as Kovis stirred again, I knew I'd run out of time to weave more narratives. I'd done all I could for him, but I still worried he might act on some latent narrative I hadn't considered.

My stomach soured at the thought. I'd done my best, but would it be enough?

Would I find him again, next sunset?

Part III: Nightmare

Sweet and Low

By Baron Tennyson and Alfred Tennyson
Lincolnshire Wake Realm

Sweet and low, sweet and low,
Wind of the western sea,
Low, low, breathe and blow,
Wind of the western sea.
Over the rolling waters go;
Come form the dying moon, and blow;
Blow him again to me,
While my little one, while my pretty one sleeps.

Sleep and rest, sleep and rest,
Father will come to thee soon;
Rest, rest on mother's breast,
Father will come to thee soon.
Father will come to his babe in the nest;
Silver sails all out of the west;
Under the silver moon,
Sleep, my little one, sleep, my pretty one, sleep.

Chapter Thirty-Two

Kovis's mood continued to trouble me. I'd done my best. There was nothing more I could do. I had to keep reminding myself of that.

After weaving our charges dreams, my siblings and I had all succumbed to exhaustion and slept a good part of the sun away, or so we learned when we woke. A late breakfast, gathered by Mema and Grandfather while we'd been slumbering, satisfied our hunger, and we reached home none the worse for wear.

The excitement had died and we'd all dispersed. I'd only just sat down on my bed again when a knock came at the door. "Come in."

The door eased open and Velma popped her head in.

I motioned her forward then patted my bed.

She sat and folded her hands. My throat constricted. She only did that when she had something important she wanted to say.

"How are you doing? That was quite an experience with Aunts." She sounded like she struggled to control her emotions.

With all the activity and my worry about Kovis, I hadn't had time to think about all that had happened, but it seemed she had.

She didn't know them like I did, so I tried to put myself in her position before responding. "It was. I was so scared." I wanted to, but didn't add that it had gotten much better.

"Ali, I want you to seriously consider something."

"What's that?"

"What Father did is inexcusable. When you wouldn't cooperate, he turned you over to them to ask them to modify your charge's timeline. You don't do that, you just don't. It's a rather extreme measure, don't you think? But judging by your general upbeat mood, you must think you've convinced them to deny Father. Ali, don't fool yourself. You're naïve if you think you have that much sway."

I wanted to object, to tell her she didn't understand, but I couldn't. "I know I'm usually too optimistic, but in this case—"

"Ali, stop. Little sister, I love you dearly, but just stop." She paused for several heartbeats probably trying to formulate a way to make me see reason. "Okay, for argument's sake let's pretend you did convince our aunts to spare Kovis. What do you think Father will do when he finds out? Look at me. Do you honestly believe he'll just let this go?"

I shook my head. She'd gotten to where I had.

"Father is never going to stop hounding you, not until… not until Kovis dies." My heart dropped at her pronouncement. "You've seen him. When he doesn't get his way, he's worse than a feral mare. He grabs on and won't let it go until he's gotten some satisfaction. Ali, I'm worried what he might do to you next."

I hadn't gotten this far in my thinking, but she was right. My heart sped. "So what do you suggest I do?" My pitch rose.

"You're not safe here anymore."

"But where would I go?"

"No, you don't understand. You're not safe in Dream realm anymore."

I stiffened. "What… what are you saying?"

Velma reached over and placed her hand on my arm. "Ali, you need to escape to Wake realm. It's the only place you can be away from him, where you'll be safe."

Going to Wake, right. I laughed. And here I'd thought she was being serious. "That's a good one, sister."

But she didn't laugh with me. She just pulled her hand back and folded them on her lap again.

I shook my head. "No, you can't be serious." But her continued stern expression told me she meant it. I furrowed my brows. "It's never been done. It's not possible."

"I'm working on a way."

I gave her a long look.

"I don't have everything figured out yet, but I'm close. I can feel it. But this is a big decision, Ali. You need time to think about it."

Think about it? No one had ever attempted what Velma suggested. I believed it was impossible, why didn't she? I was in an impossible situation, I agreed. If I stayed, Father would... My stomach clenched. I didn't want to think about it. But if I tried to flee, who knew what might happen. I opened my mouth to allow my questions to flow out, but she damned them up with two fingers to my lips.

"Think about it first. We'll talk later." She leaned over, hugged me, and rose, then sniffed and wiped her cheek as she turned. "My mind has been a whirl since we found you. This is the only way I can see to keep you safe, Ali."

I nodded as numbness overwhelmed me. I didn't even hear the door shut.

I was alone. Again.

I let my thoughts run. If I went, I wouldn't have my family anymore—not my sisters, nor my brothers, not Mema or Grandfather. Nor Mother, not that she'd been a big part, but still. My breath quickened. It'd be easier to cut off an arm or leg than lose those I loved. They were my world. My emotions rose and fell in wild succession. I felt like I was drowning. I wouldn't resurface if I didn't think of something else.

My mind slowly shifted: If I went, I'd become mortal. I'd die. And in a relatively short time. My chest started to ache. I didn't know how to even begin thinking about that. How does one with no end begin to contemplate one? What did it even mean? My charges all died. It's why they, like Kovis, all struggled with meaning. With such a short existence, every sun had to count for something, unlike with eternity. Knowing this line of thought would end equally badly, I forced myself to again think of something else.

I'd had an impact, for the better I believed, on my human charges. I'd improved their lives by diligently weaving their dreams, reorganizing their thoughts, giving them solutions to problems that thwarted them, helping them make sense of what flummoxed them, crafting narratives of meaning, and enhancing their lives in so many ways, like singing lullabies to them and more. I'd be giving all that up if I left Dream. I adored working as a sandmaiden. It brought purpose and fulfillment to my life. What would I replace it with?

This situation had arisen because Father wanted to control and possibly end Kovis. There was no way I'd let him. Ever. Not when it could lead to Father controlling Wake Realm... utterly out of the question.

I forced my thoughts to consider the positives of fleeing to Wake and a ray of light dared to show itself: If I went, I'd gain Kovis. I'd have a relationship with him. I'd fantasized about him plenty, let my thoughts run wild, even a bit obscene at times, but never once had I expected to realize any of them—I hadn't needed to actualize it to enjoy the fun. But now that I might... A slow smile built. I'd see Kovis in a way I'd not seen any of my charges before. I'd see and experience him in a way no sand person had ever experienced any dream charge. Dare I think it, a twinge of excitement ignited in my chest.

I'd build a relationship with Kovis, like those other ladies had, but I wouldn't disappoint or hurt him, ever. In fact, I'd help him flourish emotionally. I set my jaw. Yes, that would be my priority. I'd warm his heart and make it thaw. I'd help him get back to how he'd been, way back when.

My stomach fluttered as my thoughts went further. I'd get to see his beautiful eyes up close, and his muscled chest. What would it be like? I'd run my hands through his perfect brown locks and make a mess of them. I felt my cheeks warm as I wondered if we'd... be intimate. I brought a hand to my mouth and ran a finger over my lips. What did his lips feel like? What did they taste like? What might he smell like? Earthy and manly no doubt, as fitting the sensual male he'd become.

As exciting as all of this was though, my thoughts returned to my dilemma. Velma was asking me to give up my immortality and family for lasting safety... I'd gain Kovis in the process. She thought it was a worthy trade or she wouldn't have asked me to consider it.

I sighed. Love was Velma's only motivation when it came to her siblings, I knew that like I knew my name, and I had no words to describe the love she showed for me. There was always a cost to every benefit. Nothing was ever free and this might be the highest cost either of us ever had to bear... *if* I went.

Chapter Thirty-Three

"Ali's still sick," Velma insisted tonight, in the foyer. I listened from my hideaway around the corner in the private dining room.

Father fumed. His boots struck the marble floor in a regular pattern—pacing. "That's what you said last night."

"It's true. She's still unwell."

A huff, then the front door slammed, and he was gone.

I exhaled, but waited to come out lest he return. Excuses would only put him off for so long, but bless their hearts, my sisters would use every tool at their disposal to keep me away from Father. Mema helped our cause, cancelling fortnight family dinners indefinitely—we'd find other ways to keep our family close, she said.

Father had slammed his fist into the wall last night when Wynnfrith assured him I was still unwell. I'd ruffled my wings as a shudder surged down my back.

When I checked later, I found a hole in the wall.

He'd dug in. This could not end well.

"You're lying. Now get out of my way!" Father bellowed down the hallway.

"No, Father, she really is sick." Wasilla's voice hitched.

I froze where I sat on my bed.

Wynnfrith yipped on her bed across from me, wide eyed, as the sky outside pinked with the rising sun.

I knew Father would eventually explode. It'd taken a fortnight since I'd returned from my aunts, but he'd reached his limit.

Pounding. "Alissandra, open this door."

"No, don't," Wynnfrith begged as I rose.

I shook my head. "He won't be put off any longer."

Her shoulders slumped.

I opened the door.

Father's nostrils flared as he looked me up and down. "You don't look sick to me. Now, get your things and come with me."

"Ambien." Mema's voice was firm. "You cannot barge in here and take Alissandra."

"Funny, I thought I was still her father."

"This is nonsen—"

Father raised a hand. Mema silenced, but scowled beside my sisters, along with several guards who clogged the hall.

"Let... let me get ready," I said, assessing Father for how many liberties I dare take.

He nodded and I eased the door shut, then leaned against it. Wynnfrith's chin quivered.

Chaos erupted outside the door as raised voices barked protests.

I exhaled heavily. I knew what would happen if Father got riled up much more. No, I would go with him rather than see my family get hurt.

I changed back into my leather flying jacket and pants—they were getting more use than they had in a while.

Black feathers floated about when I opened the door. It had been quite the argument. Mema and my sisters all wore long faces.

"Let's go," Father said. The tone of his voice announced his annoyance.

Baldik thrust his chest out as I emerged and inserted himself between Father and me as I headed toward the stairs. Brave male.

My sisters knew not to say anything, but that didn't keep them from silently mouthing their love for me as I passed.

"Baldik and Rowntree will go with you," Mema said, striding beside me.

I raised my brows.

"Your father agreed." Mema grabbed my hand.

"Thank you." It was all I could say. It was a modest concession at best, that wouldn't stop him from doing whatever he planned, but still, it was something.

Down the stairs, through the foliage-and-fountain-filled atrium, on through the foyer, I followed Father who uttered not a word—he didn't need to. No one could miss his pissed posture.

Rowntree joined us as we headed out the front door. My guards wore leather jackets and pants similar to mine over their hulking muscular frames. As the largest guards in the palace I had no doubt why Mema had selected them for this mission. Their thumbs twitched above the swords at their sides.

The sun had just peeked above the horizon as we stepped outside. A stench hit me as five trained mares rose to their feet. I couldn't stifle my gasp as I drew a hand to cover my nose. No doubt he'd told them to wait for him there. Some, if not all, of these beasts had ensured I met my aunts.

They transformed, sprouting wings comparable to my own and together we launched, me between Rowntree and Baldik, behind Father. His trained mongrels followed, small mercy. At least I wouldn't smell them the whole way.

We headed northwest. Off to my left I surveyed Sand City that sprawled into the distance. Not only did my siblings and I enjoy spending time there, but it was just one place where the sand people our dream stitcher created, lived. It stretched farther than I could see.

The dream stitcher created sandlings who were then assigned to families to raise. When old enough, they came and received an apprenticeship in Sand City where the sand schools for our region were. When a sand being finished his or her apprenticeship, they would be assigned a human if there was a need, then return home to their assigned family. If there were enough natural sand beings at the time, they returned home until the need arose.

It was considered a huge honor to be selected to shepherd a created sandling, so adoptive families were always fighting for the opportunity. I smiled as I remembered one adoption I'd been fortunate to watch. I'd been at the sand palace when a couple came to receive their sandling. They'd beamed. They felt so honored and so proud to be chosen. They filled out various paperwork, talked to advisors, then took an oath to create a sandy environment conducive to building the best sandlings, but when they set eyes on the one they'd get to raise... My heart quickened and tears welled up once more.

A chill shimmied up my spine, bringing me back. While the ground temperature had been balmy, I was glad I had my leather jacket to cut the chilly winds as we flew over the rocky valleys, hills, and a mountain or two. Other than Porta, the tallest peak, which towered over its neighbors, the terrain was foliage-covered, but rocky, desolate, and inhospitable. Fairytales told of all manner of monsters entering Dream realm through that pinnacle, a connection with Hades itself some said, where all that was bad and evil had entered the land. Stories said Dream had been perfect before that, but evil by its very nature wanted to destroy what was good. I'd no doubt mares had been some of the mythical villains of those scary stories. I hated listening to the tales; they always set goose pimples on my arms.

Despite my family members tending toward the odd side of whatever measure you chose, it seemed they preferred to live by the coast. Whether for its moderate temperatures or the sweeping sea views, it's where they'd erected their castles—the perimeter of our island was littered with them. I spotted Uncle Tas's palace way off in the distance at one point. Like Uncle Thao, while he could be eccentric, he was harmless. But Uncle Beto's castle made the hair on the back of my neck stand up as we passed a while later. He loved scary things, especially animals. He and mares got along fabulously. My siblings and I stayed as far from him as we could.

And then, as the sun had nearly reached its peak, Father's castle came into view. The purity of its stark white walls and spires stood in contrast to who he had become—the thought sprang to mind when I saw it. Any child would willingly enter. Unfortunately, what happened on the inside... no, I wouldn't go there just yet. I'd see what he had planned. My nerves shouted that I was foolish to believe anything but the worst since I was still committed to thwarting Father's plans. I tried to hush my raging thoughts as we landed and I followed Father into his domain.

Rowntree and Baldik made it as far as the foyer before Father said, "You'll go no further. I agreed to allow you here, and I have."

They opened their mouths to object, but Father's mares lowered their heads and started growling. My guards drew their blades and took ready positions.

"Alissandra, come."

I didn't move.

My guards lunged for the enemy. They swiftly felled the first two mares who reached them with quick strokes to the neck. But the next pair of mongrels caught them recovering their balance and with a swipe of their mighty paws, downed them, then stood over, dripping saliva.

"Stop," I yelled. My brave protectors wouldn't die because of me. This wasn't worth it. Whatever Father had in mind couldn't merit their lives.

Father nodded his curs back and they obeyed, small blessing.

I'd known having guards along was a token concession. They both met my eyes with frustrated looks as I turned to follow Father. They weren't upset with me, but at their lack of effectiveness to protect their charge. It's what they'd sworn to do. I'd thwarted them, but they were alive and that's what mattered, at least to me.

Liveried stewards, who had gathered during the melee, scurried to clear the entry of the two dead mares and erase any trace of what had happened. They went about their task expeditiously and without a word. I wondered if it was a common occurrence.

Father nodded a mare to follow as he strode down one hallway, then another, toward the rear of the castle. I needed no other encouragement to keep up. My hands fidgeted despite trying to still them.

We passed Father's throne room, then the dining room, and finally entered his drawing room. His mare stopped just outside the door—I rolled my eyes, like I'd even think of running.

"Close the door, Alissandra."

As it clicked shut, Father began pacing, not saying a word. It seemed he tried to gather his thoughts. I stood silently, my nervousness migrating down my legs, making me jumpy. Back and forth he paced, between his massive ebony desk and the wall of books at the other end. His steps only amplified the backdrop of angry waves pounding the sandy shore outside.

At length, he stopped and found me standing by the door. I hadn't wanted to venture further. He schooled his expression and motioned me to sit on a divan. He was at least being civil. I crossed the room and chose to sit on the sofa farthest from him, drawing my wings in as tightly as I could. He perched on the arm of another. The short table in the center of the three sofas provided a tiny measure of moral support, creating a physical barrier to separate us. I'd take anything I could get.

"Alissandra, you are still my favorite daughter…"

His declaration shocked me. After everything I'd done, he still held me as his favorite. What if I was no longer in the favored position? Would he leave me alone?

"… so I'm choosing to try to work with you. I'd like to have you cooperate. It would be best for everyone."

Everyone but Kovis.

"You've frustrated me." He took a deep breath. "A fortnight ago, I'd had it with you."

I didn't respond.

"I appreciate your commitment to this human, but I need you to help me so I can help all humans."

"What, so you can take over Wake?" Why dance around the issue. I sounded the first blast.

"That's not what I intend."

"Then what? You tried to take over Dream, and when that didn't work, you bided your time until this opportunity appeared."

He shook his head. "Do you remember what Uncle Thao joked about during the autumn equinox celebration?"

I forced a laugh. "Yeah, that he might take over Wake one of these nights. Come on, you can't believe him, he's a crazy eccentric."

Father remained straight-faced. "You dislike the idea of me taking over Wake, imagine what would happen if *he* did? His fascination with death isn't just a pastime."

I willed my courage to endure. "If that's your true motivation, why didn't you tell me that? Why mask it behind some story about ridding humans of mares?"

He rose. I swallowed hard as he reseated himself beside me, then reached over and placed a hand on my wrist. "I never said it was. But either way, you're like your mother. Sunshine and rainbows are what suit you. You have a more delicate temperament."

Anger began to build. "Delicate?"

He patted my arm.

I yanked it out of his grasp. "If I help you, you'll still be able to bend human minds to your will."

"You trust crazy Uncle Thao more than your own father? You don't know him like I do."

His argument didn't surprise me. He blended just enough fact with fiction to accomplish his ends.

"Aunts didn't grant your request, did they?" As I'd expected, but I wouldn't tell him that. My tone had a little glee mixed in, and Father snarled. "That's why you've forced me here, isn't it?"

"Answer the question," he insisted.

I'd answer his question all right. I clenched my jaw, trying to control my temper but failed, and it poured out as I said, "After what you did to me, dragging me before my aunts, yes, I trust crazy Uncle Thao more than you."

He bolted up. "Fine. Then we'll do this the hard way."

In a heartbeat, he'd locked onto my mind like he'd done during the solstice dance and what I had believed to be experiments. But this time, it felt like he dragged sharp claws across the surface.

I moaned, grasping my head. The pain left me panting.

"Would you care to change your mind?"

I shook my head, and he again dug in.

How could I block him? The thought barely registered as pain forced another moan from me. I curled up in a ball.

"Any time you decide to help me, say the word and I'll stop." I barely made out his words as more pain shot through my head.

He paused and I panted. My head pounded, like the angry waves against the shore outside the windows.

"I'm afraid you'll need to help me; you have no choice."

"I won't sacrifice Kovis to you." I knew what my words would trigger, and he didn't disappoint. His mental claws dragged slower, but harder and I screamed.

"Damn fool." "Crazy bitch." "Whore." And worse , he called me as I dug in.

My body started trembling as he made pass after torturous pass.

"You're weak."

Slurs. They barely registered as I closed my eyes and used all my energy to cope with the pain. I wanted to, but I didn't cry. I wouldn't let myself. It would only confirm what he said.

On and on and on it went.

"You're a worthless piece of shit."

I was a worthless piece of shit. I was. No. I wasn't. Was I? Worthless shit. Worthless. Shit. Dung. Maybe I was. I was worth as much as feces.

Is this what it felt like to be broken, slowly but surely? The thought barely squeezed to the forefront of my mind.

"Stop..." It came out a whimper as I panted. My head felt like it would explode.

Father pulled back and locked eyes with me.

"I'll... I'll let you in to Kovis's mind."

"I knew you'd eventually see reason." There was no humor in his voice.

I'd let him in. But I'd never let him manipulate Kovis's thoughts. He'd have to kill me first.

I held Kovis's thought thread open to him and he availed himself of it. It took every ounce of energy that remained to keep it open. I grunted and groaned with the exertion as he took his time rooting around. Then just as my stomach threatened to empty its contents, he pulled out.

A corner of his mouth turned up. "You are stronger than I gave you credit. You may not have changed your mind about supporting my cause this sun, but I'm sure a few more times will have you seeing things differently. And by the way, should you tell anyone about this, I will know. Becoming my least favorite daughter would be unfortunate. Now get out." He turned and strode from the room.

I didn't need him to paint any pictures as to what becoming his least favorite daughter would look like. This might be bad, but that would be far worse, I had no doubt.

My head throbbed and I could barely sit up, let alone stand. But Rowntree and Baldik were at my side before I knew. They both sported slashes of red in several spots but they'd survived. They helped me up and supported me between them, practically carrying me out the front door. Rowntree took hold of me just before launching into the air.

Baldik glanced about looking for danger as we flew. Father might be fed up with me, but I had no doubt he'd change his mind about sending me away.

Chapter Thirty-Four

"Stop. What happened?" Velma demanded, where she stood, hands on hips in the foyer. Rowntree and Baldik halted at the command, supporting me between them.

I struggled to pull my head up.

"Take her to her room," Velma added.

The guards eased me onto my bed then turned and wended their way between all of my sisters who crammed into my bedroom.

"Leave us." The tone in Velma's voice left no room for debate.

The door had barely snit shut when she launched back into her story, reminding me that I needed her support. I couldn't stand up to Father alone.

I felt like a wet towel and tears flowed out unbound. It was all too much. Velma leaned over and drew me into her arms.

"We'll hide you until I figure out how to get you to Wake." Her plans spilled out, but more than that, she held me until my sobs calmed. When they had, she pulled away, looked me in the eyes, and asked, "Ali, are you with me?"

All my crying had made my headache worse, but I forced myself to think. Despite Father's verbal abuse and having his mares kidnap me and drag me before my aunts, I'd hoped he would see reason and back down in time. But from what had happened this sun, I knew I might as well hope to hold mist. Me and my damn optimism. Sunshine and rainbows, that was me.

I feared leaving Dream realm, refused to think about what life would be like without my family. Against that, giving up my immortality seemed trivial. But Velma was right, leaving Dream was the only way I'd ever be safe from Father and his schemes. My actions had all been to protect Kovis, and I still felt the rightness of it. I'd gain a much closer relationship with him in the process. I loved my family as well as Kovis, just differently, and by no means was this a trade of any kind. There was no good choice. This was just what needed to be done. I felt it in my bones.

"I'm with you," I croaked. Velma enveloped me and hugged me harder than ever. I felt tremors shake her as we cried together.

"I love you so much, Ali." Velma barely managed a whisper.

"I love you, too." The words utterly failed to convey what filled my heart toward my big sister.

Velma left me only after my reassurances that I would be okay were convincing enough.

I tossed and turned as I tried to get at least a little rest before weaving Kovis's dreams, but to no avail. While sleep abandoned me, at least my head no longer throbbed.

I exhaled, relief filling me, as I found Kovis alive and well.

Well, perhaps not well, but at least alive. His thoughts, however, continued to concern me. So much could change in a sun.

As I wove his dreams, I pictured myself as part of his life—part of his suns, not just his nights. What could I affect when I had more than his slumber to help him overcome his dark thoughts?

I finished my task and at last collapsed into an exhausted sleep of my own.

The sky was darkening as I woke. I put on a simple but comfortable dark-plum, patterned dress, preened my feathers on the wall comb, then brushed and braided my black locks. After satisfying myself that I looked presentable, I went to join Mema and my sisters for breakfast in the dining room.

But gloom had arrived before me because no one talked as I wandered in. My sisters stole looks as they ate bublik and berries, but no one seemed to want to be the first to actually talk about the situation, as if not doing so would make it go away.

A steward brought me some starfruit tea and bublik. I sat down without saying a word. I wouldn't be the first either.

Mema cleared her throat. "Ali, it goes without saying we are all heartbroken by what has happened."

I heard sniffles around the table. Phina, my next younger sister, wiped her cheek with a hanky.

"I've discussed it with your brothers, and we've decided you'll alternate staying at their palace and your grandfather and mine. It's not a perfect solution, but it will keep you safe for the time being while Velma continues her work. You'll head there after you finish weaving your charge's dreams tonight."

My stomach sank with the finality of her pronouncement.

She continued. "You have an obligation to acquire books for your aunts and deliver them in a fortnight. Perhaps your brothers have some books your aunts would enjoy. Searching out some proper books will give you something to keep yourself distracted."

My aunts and proper books, I'd have laughed had the situation not been what it was.

Velma raised a finger, and Mema yielded to her. "Ali, we need to talk after breakfast."

All I could do was nod. I had to focus on gaining Kovis. I had too or I'd shatter.

I knocked on Velma and Wasila's door some time after. Velma answered and ushered me in and invited me to sit with her on her bed. Wasila was apparently otherwise occupied because we had the room to ourselves.

"It's getting dark so we don't have much time before your charge will need you. I wanted to tell you what I'm working on since you're the one who will be impacted the most."

"Yes, good."

"You and Kovis have never been separated, you know this."

I nodded.

"When you leave Dream realm, I believe you'll sever your connection with him."

I sucked in air. "Why?"

"It's a complicated story that's not worth explaining, but the long and short of it is this. Have you ever noticed that it's easy to spot your charge out of so many humans each night when you go to him?"

"I never really thought about it, but yes, all my charge's threads have stood up when I'm near." A smile breeched my lips. "Kovis's is cute. His thought thread not only stands up, but it also waves like it wants to make sure I can't miss it."

Velma smiled in response. "That is cute. Every charge I've ever had, his or her thought thread has stood up so I could find them easily as well. Observing that got me thinking about why that is. Well, what I deduced is that the connection that begins when they are first assigned to us gives them a sensitivity to our unique presence and facilitates our nightly connections. I think of it as something akin to how any animal mother knows her baby is hers, even after being separated."

"By its unique scent."

"Exactly. Imagine how chaotic things would be if we couldn't easily find our charges every night in the mass of humanity."

"It would be a mess." I could imagine the mayhem. Humans wouldn't sleep much less dream. With a lack of rest, tensions would escalate. I shook my head. Chaos would quickly lead to destruction.

"Yes, I don't pretend to understand what that connection is; I just speculate it'll be severed. I can't see how it wouldn't. You'll be human."

I'd be human. My gaze shot to Velma. The thought hadn't occurred to me. I knew I'd become mortal, but taking on a physical body wasn't something I'd contemplated yet. What would that even be like? Everything was happening too fast.

"What will happen when our connection breaks?" The very idea sent a quiver through my stomach. Except for the mourning moon between charges, I'd always had a connection with a human. I couldn't really describe it. Whatever it was, it had made me feel responsible for each charge and filled me with a warm feeling of sorts, a feeling of belonging to someone and they to me.

"Honestly, I don't know. Hopefully nothing, but I really can't say. I wish I could."

I swallowed. I'd have to hope for the best.

"The bigger issue is what will happen *because* your connection with Kovis breaks."

"What *will* happen?"

"Never having had anyone do what you're about to, my best guess is he won't be able to sleep or dream."

"But—"

Velma waved her hands to silence me. "I'm hoping it's a simple matter of you touching him to restore sleep."

"Touching him?"

"Yes, based upon what I've worked through, I believe your touch will restore your connection, not to what it is, but to at least allow him to sleep. I believe his body will crave your touch. It's the one connection he's always known, and it will seek to restore it. I doubt he'll even understand it. I think, to him, it will be like seeking his mother's love." Velma gave me a long look. I'd told her about Kovis never knowing that love, yet he still sought it.

"How will I need to touch him?" My face warmed as I said it.

Velma caught my blush and smiled. "I think you'll enjoy it."

I threw a hand over my eyes.

Velma chuckled. "I think touching him *anywhere skin to skin* will suffice. But he won't know that." She flicked her brows.

My mouth dropped open.

Velma snickered. "A stroke of his arm perhaps, a hand to his bare chest, a kiss on his lips…"

I squeaked as her list grew. Despite the gravity of the situation, my stomach fluttered at the possibility.

"You're always bragging on Kovis. You've never said so, but I know your feelings for him have developed far beyond anything you or any of us have ever felt for another charge." My cheeks warmed. She knew. "You love him, it's clear. You no longer need to be content fantasizing." My eyes went wide. Velma laughed. "You get to go to him and realize your love. It's almost like it was meant to be."

My breath hitched. My aunts had denied having the ability to affect a human's life, but could they really? If so, had they given what had seemed a trial, to me… as a gift?

"Dreaming will require a bit more contact than sleeping," Velma added.

"More?" My eyes grew wider still.

"You spend all night with him, facilitating his dreams. It will take the same amount of time, but require physical contact to do so."

"I'll need to touch him all night?" My pitch rose.

Velma slapped her leg. "Don't tell me you never fantasized about—" She cleared her throat. "—being intimate with him. Don't you dare deny it. I'll call you a liar." She bobbed her head just once to emphasize her point.

Had I been *that* transparent? I drew a hand over my mouth to cover my grin.

"Like I said, you'll enjoy this." Velma winked.

I'd never known a male, not like that at least. My stomach fluttered. I'd seen him with women… A nervous giggle bubbled up. Would I really get to experience *all* that?

Velma looked out her window. "It's getting late. You need to go weave Kovis's dreams. I'll come find you at brothers', and we'll keep working on this."

I nodded. Velma was making this experience bearable, talking up what I could look forward to, bless her. I didn't know where I'd be without her.

Yes, *without her*... the thought brought with it a hollowness.

Chapter Thirty-Five

"How will I go to Wake realm?" My stomach clenched even as I asked, after giving her a hug the next sun.

"I'm trying to be as thorough as I can, but I know we don't have much time," Velma replied.

A couple guards had escorted me to the palace of sand men after weaving Kovis's dreams, and she'd flown here to keep my whereabouts secret. I'd head to Mema and Grandfather's place after our meeting and weaving Kovis's dreams tonight.

I'd gotten a little sleep in a spare bedroom my brothers had tried to pretty up for me on short notice, but Velma looked a bit worse for wear with circles darkening the space under her eyes.

The sun was still above the horizon so we had time to work on questions like this that had been interrupting my sleep. Her forced smile told me the same questions were also the cause of her lack of sleep.

"Ali, I'm not going to honey coat things. You know it's never been done. I'm doing everything I can to ensure you make it safely, but there's a chance you might die in the transition."

"I thought you'd figured out how to send me."

"I believe I have, but there are always risks. You don't have a choice, little sister. At the rate Father's going, he'll deliver you to the gates of Hades itself for eternal damnation."

My stomach tightened despite knowing as much. I took a deep breath. She was doing her best; I'd do mine and help by supporting and encouraging her.

"Ashes to ashes, dust to dust. You've heard humans refer to that when one of them dies. I got to thinking about that, and it led me to reflect on their creation story," she said. "I believe it hints at how to send you to Wake."

I lifted a brow to her.

"Hear me out. You know it, but let me refresh your memory and I think you'll see: In the beginning, the Ancient One gathered sand, dust, and ashes and mixed them together in the caldron of the skies. He envisioned his creation as beautiful and fruitful and everything he loved, then breathed over the great cauldron with a breath of wind. A sandstorm erupted and it shaped and molded the contents. He tipped it over, and humans, animals, sea creatures, every living thing poured out. The unformed extra material he tossed into the skies and it became stars, which he breathed on too, making them twinkle and smile upon humans.

"He decided humans needed magic so he breathed again. His breath struck the ground and carved a canyon. The ground was overwhelmed by his power and much of it embedded itself. To this sun, that landmark still radiates his power. This is how he gave magic to humans.

"Knowing humans would need guidance, the Ancient One then created Dream realm to steward his creation. But he grinned. With the free will he'd given them, he knew they wouldn't take kindly to being guided—they'd see Dream as shackles of a sort, rise up and try to throw off their seeming bonds. So he decided he wouldn't tell them, and he hid Dream behind a thick canopy."

"You really believe all this?" I asked.

"Before all this happened, I'd never really thought about it. It was just a story we'd all heard since we were young."

"But it doesn't say anything about going to Wake."

Velma smiled. "I didn't see it either, at first. Let me walk you through what I've deduced."

I held my breath. She loved me dearly; I didn't doubt that at all. And as a result, she didn't want harm to come to me. But I'd be entrusting my life to whatever she'd come to understand.

"What does it say the Ancient One did?" she asked.

I thought for a heartbeat. "He envisioned his creation as beautiful and fruitful and everything he loved, then breathed."

Velma nodded. "How do we weave dreams?"

"I envision reaching out to the dream canopy, then imagine soaring down to find my charge. I find his thought thread and get to work."

"Exactly, and what is envisioning?"

"Thinking how you want something to be."

"Yes, it's thinking the words in our minds and then willing it to be."

"Okay." I wasn't quite grasping her meaning.

She continued, "I believe I can envision transforming you into a human and sending you to your charge. I think if I then breathe over you, you will transform and find him. I don't pretend to know exactly how it works, but it clearly did during creation, and I believe magic still exists."

I gave her a long look. "But you're not a god. You don't have that kind of power."

"I'm not so sure."

I gave her a long look.

She held up a hand. "If you interpret the story literally, I agree, I don't have that kind of power. But what if the *narrative* I envision is where the power lies?"

I cocked my head.

"Hear me out. We transform our charges thoughts by simply changing their narratives all the time. What if language is where the power lies? The language we use has the power to shift our charges perspectives, their very realities. I believe the creation story is more than a story of how things became physically. I believe it's also a tale of how things can be transformed with language, which we each possess—that's where the power lies. We just don't perceive it. Like Dream being hidden from humans so they wouldn't revolt against us, what if the Ancient One hid the power of language from us so we wouldn't misuse it?"

I considered Velma's argument, and the longer I did, the more merit I found to it. I'd modified the narratives of all of my charges, significantly improving their lives. It wasn't the magic that Wake had, but it was a magic of sorts. And pretty powerful at that. No, I'd never physically transformed anything, but I'd never thought to.

"Ali, if this works like I think it will, I won't know what your new body looks like much less be able to find you, so this can't be undone."

I sucked in a breath and clasp my hands, trying, and failing, to still them.

This. Had. Never. Been. Done.

So much could go wrong. It was Velma, but still.

I took a deep breath. She was doing her best, for me.

But. This. Had. Never. Been. Done.

I couldn't silence my mind.

I could die!

Chapter Thirty-Six

I'd successfully hidden, moving between locations, for a fortnight. I wanted to believe I'd successfully evaded Father but a nagging feeling of impending doom refused to quiet.

Kovis's thoughts still troubled me, but I believed I'd gotten him past the worst of his despair although I still had work to do concerning his frozen heart. I started believing perhaps I wouldn't need to go, even though I'd warmed to and even accepted the possibility. It would be fun to see how close I could become to Kovis.

I'd spent the sun at Grandfather and Mema's place, but I'd risen early and decided to join my sisters for breakfast. Believing everything was at peace once more, Grandfather decided to go spend the sun up at his man cave on the northeast coast. Mema had frowned. She knew he'd end up spending not just one, but several suns there, for once he fell asleep, it was nigh impossible to wake him. Yes, he was loving retirement. I'd chuckled. They were so cute together.

Mema and I flew home, accompanied by two guards for safe measure. It was dark by the time we landed, but we were just in time for fairy dust pancakes. Apparently Mema had arranged the surprise with the kitchen unbeknownst to my sisters. My visit being unexpected, the heartbeat we walked into the dining room, Wasila, Ailith, Phina, all my sisters really, pushed away from the table squealing and engulfed me in hugs. Mema smiled and didn't reprimand them, enjoying the warmth we all shared.

As Wynnfrith held me, she said, "It's too quiet in our room without you."

"I miss you too, big sister."

It felt so good to be held, hugged, supported. No matter what happened, I would never forget this feeling.

We finished breakfast when the unmistakable stench of a mare wafted through the dining room doors. We all looked around, but before I could rise, much less hide, Father stood in the doorway, a mare on either side.

His stiff posture hushed all conversation, as well as any objection about him bringing mares in the house. His jaw clenched as he stared daggers at me. I clutched the edge of the table.

"Alissandra." His voice was cold and my hands turned sweaty. I should have known he'd find me if I dared come here. He probably had a mare or two watching for when I finally showed up.

"You *will* cooperate, this is my last warning."

I swallowed hard, then sat up straight. "No, I won't."

The look that crossed his face... I hoped I'd never see it again.

"You can't have Kovis's mind. I won't let you."

"We'll see about that."

If I were going to go down in flames, I'd do it big. I set my jaw, infuriating Father even more, and rose. "You think making humans lose their sense of self-awareness and identity, making them always sleep and care only for what you tell them to, no matter what the circumstances or cost to them, will benefit them?"

"Your uncle has threatened to kill them all. They're better off catatonic than dead."

"They might as well be dead if that's the extent of their existence. You tried to take over Dream and now you're after Wake."

Father lunged for me. I couldn't get clear of his grasping hands, and he captured me. He squeezed my arms, his grip growing tighter the more I struggled—I feared they'd break. His face shriveled in an ugly snarl as he shook me.

I whimpered, but the mares at his sides ensured no one helped me.

"Stop your damn whimpering."

I could only whimper more.

He grew frustrated and pressed my face into his fatty chest. I couldn't breathe and I struggled to move my head. Air. I needed air. I pushed, then clawed at his tunic. One of my nails found the open placket and drew blood. I flailed my wings. It only fanned his anger hotter.

Father captured one of my wings and stilled it in his vice grip. From the corner of my eye, I saw a blade appear in his hand. How? I beat my wings faster as he brought that blade up. He would shred them. *Dyeus, stop him.* But Dyeus ignored me.

I hit and scratched his chest harder making him loosen his grip just enough for me to suck in air. I had to get free. His nipple. The disgusting thing stuck out not far away. My feet were still on the floor and I pushed up with all the strength I could muster until my nose brushed against the bulbous thing. I didn't think. I opened my mouth and, in a heartbeat, clamped down through his tunic.

"Damn! Stupid bitch!" Father thrust me a good distance, into the wall.

I hit my head and crumpled to the floor as stars filled my vision.

Run! My mind instinctively knew this would be my only chance because, with my luck, if he caught me, he'd do worse than try to kill me. He'd damn me to Hades itself.

I scrambled up, taking wobbly strides as my head cleared.

He shouted more obscenities as he nursed his bleeding chest.

I raced out the door.

"Quickly, follow me." Velma grabbed my hand as I barreled down the hall, her eyes never stopping their search for enemies.

"Alissandra." Father's bellow shook the walls behind us.

We flew down one hall after the next; Father's raging never far behind.

Velma finally fluttered into a small alcove, panting. "Ali, we've talked about this."

I nodded, shaking.

"It's time for you to go, little sister." She struggled to catch her breath.

"I'm scared," I cried.

"I know you are, but it's the only way you'll be safe."

I choked back tears.

"Be brave. It's better to give up immortality and make a life for yourself. You love Kovis. You've put yourself in jeopardy for him. Now go and make a happy life with him."

I hugged her. "I love you." Tears breached the dam I'd held them behind.

Velma looked into my eyes as tears trickled down her cheeks, too. "And I love you. Now go and be safe."

Father bellowed, too close.

Velma gripped my shoulders, closed her eyes, then breathed over me.

How I prayed this worked, because I didn't want to die.

Ali's story continues in Good Night, the third book in The Sand Maiden series! Buy it now at smarturl.it/Buy_GoodNight

Buy at Amazon Now!
smarturl.it/Buy_GoodNight

Please Leave a Review

Did you, your Sand Man, or Sand Maiden enjoy the Prequel? Share your thoughts in a quick review on Amazon. It can be as short as a sentence! You can make a huge difference.
smarturl.it/Review_RABB

_____

FaceBook Fan Group

Did you have an emotional rollercoaster ride reading this book? Do you need others to talk to about it?
https://www.facebook.com/groups/LRWLeeStreetTeam/
All the feels and fanning you can handle!

_____

Stay Informed!

There are more books in The Sand Maiden trilogy.
To instantly receive notice when L. R. W. Lee releases the next one or has news about other upcoming events, sign up
http://www.lrwlee.com/na-fantasy-romance-signup

_____

Other Books by L. R. W. Lee

Be sure to check out L. R. W. Lee's award-winning, seven book, coming-of-age, epic fantasy series

Andy Smithson

Download the book for free from Amazon now at
http://smarturl.it/BoDF

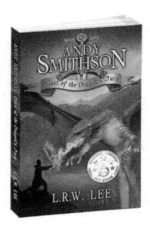

Video games don't train you to fight dragons!

Andy Smithson just found out how much the zap of a wizard's curse can sting. But after an epically bad day, he finds wizards are the least of his problems.

An otherworldly force draws him to a medieval world where fire-breathing dragons, deranged pixies, and vengeful spirits are the way of things. Trading his controller for a sword of legend, Andy embarks upon an epic quest to break a centuries-old curse oppressing the land. It isn't chance that plunges him into the adventure though, for he soon discovers ancestors his parents have kept hidden from him are behind the curse.

Blast of the Dragon's Fury is a coming-of-age, epic fantasy adventure featuring fast-paced action, sword fights, laugh-out-loud humor, with a few life lessons thrown in.

Download the book for free from Amazon now at
http://smarturl.it/BoDF

Connect with L. R. W. Lee

BookBub has a New Release Alert. Not only can you check out my latest deals, but you can also get an email when I release my next book, by following me here:
https://www.bookbub.com/profile/l-r-w-lee

http://www.LRWLee.com
https://www.facebook.com/lrwlee
https://www.instagram.com/lrwlee/
https://www.pinterest.com/lindarwlee/
https://www.twitter.com/lrwlee
https://www.goodreads.com/author/show/7047233.L_R_W_Lee

——————

Acknowledgements

Special thanks to my Beta readers Rachel Rousseau, Cait Jacobs, Erica Sebree and Kirstyanne Ross who provided lots and lots of constructive feedback for Rock-A-Bye Baby in its most formative stages. You all are troopers to have waded through the initial swamp. LOL.

But there are four additional Beta readers who caused me to up my game: Alicia Logsdon, Kathleen Lightfoot, Lauren Rebecca Hassen, and Le Good. Ladies, you truly inspired me to make this book the best it could possibly be. You challenged me to tell Ali's story in a way that readers would not just understand, but love, and cheer her on to victory. You made me stretch. Boy, did you ever. You're a tough bunch, but I thank you for it. Rock-A-Bye Baby is better because of you.

Thanks also to my Merry Mayhem Makers who moderate the

Facebook Fan Group—Claire Manuel, Courtney Belaire, Georgina Gallacher, Kiersten Burke, and Samantha Zeman. You all haven't technically been together in this capacity for long, but from the conversations we have you'd never know it. Thank you so much for your dedication. You are a source of fun, inspiration, warmth, and encouragement and I'm having a ball hanging out with you all.

Appendix

Time designations:
Sun – a day
Sennight – a week, or seven suns
Fortnight – two weeks
Moon – a month
Annum – a year

A day in Wake is like a day on Earth:
Morning – breakfast
Evening – dinner

A day in Dream is opposite a day on Earth:
They sleep while the sun is up and work while it's dark.

Breakfast - They have breakfast as the sun sets because they have slept through the day and just risen, in time to weave the dreams of their charges, as they sleep.

Dinner - They have dinner as the sun is rising, after a full night of work weaving their charges dreams is done.

Printed in Great Britain
by Amazon